"We Need To Talk."

Those four little words lay heavy with meaning, conjuring up a multitude of awkward scenarios from Kat's disastrous past. Ten weeks ago, they'd not only crossed that line between friends and lovers, they'd burned it to the ground, and part of her wanted to run home and hide under the bed covers.

"About?"

"We can talk on my boat."

She sighed. "Look, Marco, it's late and there's a cyclone approaching. Can't this wait another day?"

"You've been avoiding my calls, so no. And the storm's not due for hours yet."

He glanced up at the dark sky, narrowed his eyes at the barely discernible wind that had picked up.

"I'm tired."

He stared at her, irritated. "Phone calls. Avoiding."

She blinked slowly. "You're not going to give up until I agree, are you?"

"No."

"Dammit, you can be sooooo annoying!"

"Says the woman who still hasn't told me she's pregnant."

* * *

Dear Reader,

I've made a major discovery (well, two) about my writing self this last year. One, I can pretty much write anywhere, even with screaming children and noisy machinery in the background, as long as I have an excellent pair of noise-cancelling headphones and music. And two—if the hero isn't right in my mind, if he isn't larger than life, in my face and demanding his story be told, the book doesn't work.

Marco from *Suddenly Expecting* was such a man. Originally appearing in *Bed of Lies* as hero Luke's cousin, he demanded his own story and at the time I thought I knew the perfect woman for him. Boy, was I wrong! I was also wrong about what he looked like and went through a few different faces to finally land on the perfect guy for Kat, my heroine. (You can read about it all on my blog!) At the time of writing I was also listening to a lot of baroque music, and my favorite composer just had to get a mention in there. And of course, it wouldn't be one of my books without setting it in towns I know and love— this time Cairns, Sydney and Brisbane.

I'd love to hear what you think of Kat and Marco's story! You can visit me at www.paularoe.com.

Love, Paula x

SUDDENLY
EXPECTING

—

PAULA ROE

H HARLEQUIN® DESIRE

Recycling programs
for this product may
not exist in your area.

ISBN-13: 978-0-373-73304-0

SUDDENLY EXPECTING

Copyright © 2014 by Paula Roe

Printed in U.S.A.

Books by Paula Roe

Harlequin Desire

Bed of Lies #2142
A Precious Inheritance #2186
The Pregnancy Plot #2268
Suddenly Expecting #2291

Silhouette Desire

Forgotten Marriage #1824
Boardrooms & A Billionaire Heir #1867
The Magnate's Baby Promise #1962
The Billionaire Baby Bombshell #2020
Promoted to Wife? #2076

Other titles by this author available in ebook format.

PAULA ROE

Despite wanting to be a vet, choreographer, card shark, hairdresser and an interior designer (although not simultaneously!), British-born, Aussie-bred Paula ended up as a personal assistant, office manager, software trainer and aerobics instructor for thirteen interesting years.

Paula lives in western New South Wales, Australia, with her family, two opinionated cats and a garden full of dependent native birds. She still retains a deep love of filing systems, stationery and traveling, even though the latter doesn't happen nearly as often as she'd like. She loves to hear from her readers—you can visit her at her website, www.paularoe.com.

This story required an extra kick in the pants and I truly appreciate kickers Shannon Curtis and Kaz Delaney for doing that. You know how much I love you girls xx Huge cuddles to Helene Young for her wonderful cyclone information, and Gabrielle Luthy for her knowledge of all things French. And a special thanks to Kaycie from the Football Federation of Australia who went over and above to provide this soccer-challenged writer with information regarding the sport.

I also need to mention some special characters in Twitter Land who for one reason or another provided either encouragement or sweet, hilarious distraction throughout this particular story and kept this writer sane: George IV, Will Shakespeare, Prince Henry, Jack Sheppard, Philippe and Charles Brandon. Love you, guys! Lastly, to the wonderful, gorgeous people behind the epic French movie *Le Roi Danse*. Because period dramas totally rock.

One

Ten weeks ago, Katerina Jackson had spent one night in bed with her best friend. And it had been absolutely amazing.

Now, as she drove down the Captain Cook Highway, just before she got into Cairns, she was confronted with an image of the man in question, naked and smiling seductively down at her.

Kat's foot instinctively tamped on the brake, and she only just managed to avoid the car in front as it stopped at the red light. The burn on her cheeks went all the way down her body, ending in her thighs, where it pooled annoyingly in her groin. She looked up at the familiar massive billboard featuring Marco Corelli, the golden boy of France's premier *futball* league and Marseille's highest goal scorer in the club's entire history.

Well, he wasn't exactly naked. The stacked Y-fronts

left little to the imagination, though, as did his splayed hands across his low-riding waistband and the caption "Come and Feel My Skins." But it wasn't his ridged abs, popping biceps and the seductive Adonis line of muscle that disappeared into the low-riding underwear that heated her blood. It was that familiar, tempting come-here-so-I-can-have-my-way-with-you grin, the curve of his overtly lush bottom lip and the forbidden promise in those dark, sensual eyes. The way the camera had captured his hypnotic charm as he looked up from behind artfully tousled, rakish black hair, one curl lying teasingly across his forehead and cheek.

She'd had to pass that damn billboard every morning for the past ten weeks, his perfect face staring knowingly down, as if he remembered every single thing he'd done to her that night. How he'd made her sweat, how he'd made her moan. How he'd made her pant.

She snapped her gaze back to the road, glaring at the taillights as the traffic finally began to move.

"God, I am so stupid," she muttered in the air-conditioned silence. It was Marco, her best friend since high school. The arrogant former-soccer-star-turned-sports-commentator, the underwear-endorsing charmer, Mr. Flirt with a dozen different girlfriends. She was his best mate, secret keeper, sounding board, partner in crime. His plus one when he needed a date to some swish function. He was also her boss's on-again, off-again boyfriend.

She cast her mind back, sifting through her and Grace's many conversations about Marco. Yeah, they'd definitely been off for a while before that night, so there was one less moral dilemma to worry about. Which just left the main two.

Oh, she couldn't just have sex with her best friend, noooo. She had to end up pregnant, too.

If you could see me now, Mum. All your pretty, shiny dreams of your daughter having a perfect life, a perfect career. A perfect husband surrounded by perfect, healthy children.

The sliver of pain sliced through her, drawing blood, before she effectively sealed up the wound and pulled into Channel Five's parking lot. After flashing her ID to the guard, she parked, gathered her bag and strode into the studio. Then she tossed her bag in her office and checked her phone.

Four missed calls, one from her friend Connor, three from Marco, plus a text message. Back in town. We need to talk. Drinks on the boat? M x

She sighed then finally replied. Sorry, snowed under at work. Can't get away. Plus there's a cyclone warning, in case you haven't noticed. K x

After she sent it, she scrolled back to their texts from two months ago, a painful reminder that only rekindled her inner turmoil.

Have a good trip to France.

Hate to run and fly. We shouldn't leave last night without talking about it.

Nothing to say. Let's just blame it on booze and stupidity and forget it happened, okay?

Are you cool with that?

Totally. Erasing from my memory in three...two...one...

☺ Okaaaay. See you in a few weeks.

And that was it. Due to both their schedules, they had a mutual phone blackout during his assignments, although he always managed to send a few photos of the local scenery. But now he was back and wanted to do the usual drink-and-talk, and she had no idea what to tell him.

You can't avoid him forever.

"You can't avoid him forever," Connor confirmed five minutes later when she returned his call.

"What the hell, I'm gonna give it a shot."

"Don't be ridiculous. He deserves to know."

Kat slid her hip on the corner of her desk and sighed. "I can hear your disapproval all the way from Brisbane."

"Kat, I'm not disapproving. But I'm one of the few who know exactly what you've gone through these past few years. The guy deserves to know."

Trust Connor to tell it to her straight. Marco, Connor, Kat and Luke—the Awesome Foursome, they'd called themselves in high school. All so very different in personality and temperament, yet "perfectly awesome together," as Marco had put it. He'd been the cocky one, a skilled charmer, whereas his cousin Luke had had the whole bad-boy thing going on, always in trouble, always on detention. Connor was the devastatingly handsome silent-and-deep one, her unbiased sounding board who always told her the truth, uncolored by hyperbole or emotion. Sometimes it was scary how detached he could actually be, which was, ironically, what made him an exceptional businessman. He never let anyone into his private circle and she was always grateful she'd been allowed entry all those years ago.

"I…just can't tell him," she said now. "I'm already a wreck, and I can't deal with all the emotional baggage, too."

"That's unfair, sweetie. Marco would never do that to you."

She pinched the bridge of her nose and then glanced up as a runner gave her the wind-up signal, indicating she was due on set.

Kat nodded. "Look, I have to go. I'll talk to you later."

Connor sighed. "Stay safe during the storm."

"I will." She hung up, firmly pushed the conversation to one side and made her way to makeup just as her phone rang again.

It was Marco. "I do *not* want to talk to you," she muttered and slid the phone to Silent.

"Avoiding a call from the boyfriend?"

Kat slid a glance to Grace Callahan, the star of Queensland's number one breakfast chat show, *Morning Grace,* sitting in the makeup chair, getting her hair done. The woman was forty, only seven years older than Kat, but she had that polished, shiny look of someone who'd not only spent enormous amounts of time and money on her appearance, but was convinced it was the most important thing in her life. Her blond hair was curled into an artful tousle, her fake-tanned skin smooth, her body gym-honed. Yet for all her high-maintenance appearance, she had an addictive personality that attracted people by the bucket load. Which was probably why Marco kept coming back.

Kat glanced at her phone and nodded, unwilling to explain further. "No, just…a guy."

"Really?" Grace's wide eyes met hers in the mirror. "A real-life guy? Oh, my God, where's my phone? I want to take a picture of this moment."

Despite her mood, Kat smiled. "You make me sound like a nun."

"I was beginning to think you were, hon." She winced as the makeup girl pulled a lock of hair through the curler. "This is exciting—makes a change from all the Cyclone Rory news. Can I put it in the show?"

Kat snorted a laugh. "You know you can't, so stop asking. I'm not newsworthy."

"Are so." Grace waved the girl away and ripped the makeup cape from her shoulders. "You're a celebrity, and celebrities are always news."

"Please, don't remind me. I hate those people who're famous for just being famous."

"Sorry, hon, but your little scandals have fueled the gossip columns for ages. It only takes another to set it off again." She straightened her dress then walked to the door, Kat following.

Kat sighed. It was true. She was nothing particularly special: the daughter of a merchant investment banker and an events planner, a private school student. The gap year she'd spent between high school graduation and university had been twelve months of partying, but just as she was about to begin her journalism degree at Brisbane Uni, she'd been offered a job as society reporter for *The Tribune* instead. Then, she'd gone spectacularly off the rails a year later, after her mother's death.

"You never did set the record straight about everything, you know," Grace said over her shoulder as they continued down the corridor. "It'd make a fabulous feature." She swept her hands out, indicating a huge headline. "Former It Girl Katerina Jackson finally spills the dirt on her marriages, the seedy side of French football and *those* scandalous photos."

"Never going to happen, Grace."

"We could start at the beginning, make it a full show. We'd do background, talk about your childhood, your upbringing. How you beat up Marco when you were fourteen—"

"It was a shove, not a hit—"

"—and how you all ended up on detention like some modern-day *Breakfast Club* scenario—"

"I *knew* I shouldn't have told you that."

Grace laughed. "I'm not going to say anything, hon, unless you want me to. But I do find it fascinating that your closest friends are a soccer superstar, a billionaire merchant banker and the nephew of a rumored mobster. All hot alpha men. All completely different. And all newsworthy."

Marco, Connor and Luke. Her best friends since high school, since that awkwardly hilarious lunchtime detention had played out like some eighties teenage movie and they'd bonded over their hatred of school and their shared tastes in movies, music and computer games.

"What were you all there for again?" Grace casually asked as they walked to the studio.

"You know full well what."

"You'd decked Marco—"

"A *shove,* Grace. For showing off in front of his mates and getting all up in my face."

"Why? What did he say?"

"Honestly, I can't even remember." Yeah, she did —a stupid teenage comment about her lack of "womanly attributes" that, to Marco's credit, he'd apologized for later.

"Whatever. Luke had been caught defacing the toilets and… What was Connor's crime?"

"Correcting the economics teacher then threatening to bankrupt him."

"Wow, harsh."

"That was Southbank Private for you." She shrugged. "All the girls were too intimidated to talk to Luke and Connor. I wasn't. And from there we clicked. It just so happens they're guys."

"And you've never thought about…?" Grace waggled her eyebrows. *You know.*

"What? No!"

"Not even with Marco?"

Kat threw her an exaggerated eye roll to cover up the warmth in her face. "No, Grace, I haven't," she replied as they walked onto the set. "And I have no intention of giving anyone an exclusive. I'm your research assistant now, that's it." Grace approached a raised yellow couch and coffee table surrounded by a cluster of cameras. The lights streamed down as the set director came over to go through the lineup. "The other stuff is old news. People don't want to hear about it."

"They do. But I'll just keep trying," Grace replied with a smile, taking the glass of water the runner offered.

"Of course you will." Kat accepted her usual green tea from the set assistant as Grace sat on the sofa and began to rearrange the strategically placed props on the table.

"Soooo…have you heard from Marco?" Grace asked casually.

"Not yet, no," Kat lied, fiddling with her phone. "He

was commentating the *Coupe de France,* and that was only three days ago."

"I heard he's supposed to be back today." She smoothed her dress down over her artfully crossed legs. "I'm arranging a surprise dinner for later in the week."

"Really?" Kat paused, her insides suddenly tight, and she took a sip of tea to cover up the weird feeling. "Are you two back on again, then?"

Grace laughed. "I don't think we've ever really been off. I've got plans." She took another sip of water. "Let's face it—my body clock's been ticking steadily for years. And now I have an established show and some serious credibility in this industry. It's time I started thinking about having a baby."

Kat choked, tea dribbling down her chin. She swiped at it then stared at Grace. "With *Marco?*"

"Of course with Marco!" Grace frowned slightly, eyeing the guy adjusting the lighting. "Is that a problem? I know you and he are close…"

"Oh, no. I mean, yes… I mean…" Kat took a breath, trying to steady her clenching gut. "We're close and share a lot, but we do have one rule—never butt into each other's love life."

"Really?" Grace looked intrigued. "So he's never commented on James or Ezio, not even in passing?"

"No."

"And you've never said anything to him about me?"

Kat gave her a look. "No. It's not my business. You want to have babies, it's fine with me." She gave a smile, one she'd learned to adopt out of necessity. A smile designed for intrusive cameras, when they'd been camped outside her door, trailing her on the way to work, shopping, to the gym, interrupting her family and friends and becoming so invasive she'd had to get a court order to put a stop to it.

"You sure?" Grace asked curiously as she gathered up her notes. "I always thought there was some subtle sexual tension going on with you guys, but—"

"Me and Marco? No. No way!" she denied, a little too forcefully. "I mean, he's a great-looking guy and he's my best friend, but he's…" She groped for a word. "A free spirit."

"I would've said a tart," Grace added with a smile. "And a world-class flirt. A good thing, too—he won't butt into my life and make demands on how I should be raising my child."

What could she say to that? Everything Grace said was true. Marco loved his life and lived it at breakneck speed. He had no room for a permanent partner, let alone a child.

Kat swallowed thickly, watching everyone fuss around Grace as the cameras got into position. For all her confusion, her crazy thoughts and outrageous scenarios she'd gone through these past few days, the choice was simple. He wouldn't want a baby. She most certainly didn't.

Kat adjusted her headset and sidestepped the studio camera as it wheeled toward her, watching Grace smiling into Camera One as she continued with her dialogue.

Grace could be snippy, snarky and demanding, but beneath the polished blond exterior she had a heart of gold. Kat sourced the hard-luck stories and Grace reported them, raising thousands for each charity they publicized. Grace was the public face, the ex-soapie star clawing her way back from alcohol and drugs to become the biggest-rating breakfast talk show in Queensland. Kat preferred it like that, preferred to work behind the scenes. It made a nice change, even though she still fielded a handful of interview requests every day.

No, she was content with her life. Work filled every waking moment, which meant no time for dating. Just as she'd told Connor during their regular "bon voyage, Marco" night out ten weeks ago in a Brisbane bar, she didn't do attachments or relationships anymore.

"Too much work, too difficult to navigate and way too painful when they inevitably end," she'd said, downing her drink and eyeing her friends across the table.

Marco and Luke had laughed, but Connor had had a weird look, a kind of sad-but-deadly-serious one that had annoyed her enough to order that last, fateful vodka and orange.

She swallowed an irritating lump in her throat. There was nothing wrong with her. As a teenager she'd never been obsessed with boyfriends, weddings or babies, which had set her apart from most girls in the elite Southbank Private School in Brisbane. Couple that with her preference for sport, pub bands and getting dirty over short skirts, makeup and gossip, and she'd naturally migrated toward the boys. And then there was "that incident"—as her father had called it—when she'd shoved Marco Corelli, the son of the now-notorious crime boss Gino Corelli. After the furor had died down and she'd done her counseling and detention stint, she'd realized she'd become a bit of a legend to her peers. Connor Blair, the moody silent one, had allowed her to sit with them at lunch. Luke—always so very angry—had bonded with her over obscure pub bands, and Marco… Well, he'd apologized and she'd scored a friend for life.

Complicated, complex Marco. The cocky, flirty teenager with an insane gift for soccer, who'd grown up into a gorgeous, talented, self-assured man. The guy knew her secrets, her childhood wishes, her family tragedies.

Especially her family tragedies. With her mother's death from motor neuron disease and the chances of Kat being a carrier, she'd never allowed that particular fantasy of becoming a mother take root. But now, faced with the bald-faced reality of actually being pregnant, she had absolutely no clue how to feel. After all those years of refusing the tests, of arguing with Marco that she preferred to spend her life living and not worrying, she'd actually gone and gotten tested. Now she had to wait for the results, which added extra stress to her already stressful situation.

Which was why she couldn't tell Marco. Ever.

With a sigh, she refocused on the here and now. By the time they'd finished filming the week's shows, it was eleven at night and Kat was dead on her feet. She said good-night to everyone and dragged herself to her car, fumbling with the keys as she went, her mind focused on takeout, a hot bath and double-checking her apartment for the impending storm.

Then she glanced at her car and stopped in her tracks.

Marco.

Her heart pounding, her gaze swept over him—his suit, his loosened tie, the dark hair flopping over his forehead and curling at the collar. The faint shadow of stubble dusting his firm jaw. The way he stood, all sexy and casual, hands buried in his pockets. And those wide, piercing brown eyes staring straight at her.

On another man, one with less confidence and overt sexuality, his features could almost be called pretty, if not for the overabundant aura of pure male surrounding him. His hair was a controlled crop of curls, perfectly framing those high cheekbones, lush mouth and come-to-bed eyes. And when he smiled…Lord, you could hear the knickers dropping for miles around. He reminded her of days gone by, of stocking-and-breech-clad heroes, flamboyant coats and huge romantic gestures full of wild symphonies and desperate, love-smitten poems.

And he'd been the best sex she'd had in her life.

Yes, he was adored by millions around the world. Everyone knew the story—only son of Italian immigrants, raised in Australia until a talent scout had recruited him for the French *futball* league at the tender age of sixteen. Marco, the dreamy Italian with romantic eyes and glorious touch-me hair. If that wasn't enough of an unfair advantage, he'd also acquired a hot French accent from his years living and working in Marseille and Paris. Marco, her best friend.

Her heart contracted then expanded again, and she wanted to die from the sudden ache of it all.

They'd known each other for nearly twenty years. Telling him would irrevocably change everything. Marco didn't do commitment. He loved his job, he loved women and he loved the freedom to enjoy both. And there was no way she'd lose him as her best friend after one foolish—*amazing*—night. She couldn't.

With a deep breath she continued, heading straight for her car. And the closer she got, the worse the weird feeling grew.

They'd done things—intimate things. Things she'd never imagined doing with him. They'd gotten naked, and he'd touched her and kissed her all over. Now he wanted to talk about it, and she'd rather swim with a pod of sharks than rehash her supreme stupidity that involved *that night*.

God, could it get any worse? With false bravado, she clicked off her car alarm and then crossed the last few meters to open the door.

"What are you doing here?" she asked, resisting the urge to lay a hand on her belly. Instead, she tossed her bag into the passenger seat.

"We need to talk." His unique voice—a sexy mix of French and faint Italian accents—never failed to make her shiver, but now she shoved her hair back behind her ear and steeled herself to face him. The bright security lights slashed across his face, revealing a serious expression that made her heart thump. But instead of giving in to the panic, she swallowed and crossed her arms, tilting her head.

"About?"

"We can talk on my boat."

She sighed. "Look, Marco, it's late and there's a cyclone approaching. Can't this wait another day?"

"You've been avoiding my calls, so no. And the storm's not due for hours yet."

He glanced up at the dark sky and narrowed his eyes at the barely discernible wind that had picked up.

"I'm tired."

He stared at her, irritated. "Phone calls. Avoiding."

She blinked slowly. "You're not going to give up until I agree, are you?"

"Non."

She sighed. "Fine. But be quick about it."

He eased off her car, moving into her personal space, and instinctively Kat took a step back, which only prompted him to frown. "You're not going to stand me up, are you?"

"No, I am not. Girl Guide's honor."

"Good." With a firm nod, he walked past her, got in his car and drove off.

She watched his taillights blink as he turned left out of the parking lot before she had time to fully comprehend what her acquiescence really meant.

We need to talk. Those four little words lay heavy with meaning, conjuring up a multitude of awkward scenarios from her disastrous past. Ten weeks ago, they'd not only crossed that line between friends and lovers, they'd burned it to the ground, and part of her wanted to run home and hide under the bedcovers. The other part wanted this awkward situation over and done with.

With a sigh she got in her car, fired up the engine and drove out of the car park. She couldn't run from him forever. It was time to suck it up and face whatever consequences that one night had wrought.

The marina was alive with activity, crowded with people securing their boats and belongings in preparation for the oncoming storm. Kat parked and headed down the wooden platform, eyeing the foreboding water as the dark waves lapped against the jetty. In a few hours' time, a category-four cyclone would sweep across the coast, and everyone knew all too well the devastation it would bring. The city had only just managed to recover after Cyclone Yasi had slammed into North Queensland some years before.

Marco's boat was moored at the end, a sleek, shiny thing he'd gone into great loving detail about when he'd first bought it. The only thing she remembered from that conversation was not the horsepower, the dimensions or the fuel consumption, but rather his little-kid excitement. It had made her heart flip then, as it did now when she recalled the three-year-old memories.

He stood on the deck and offered his hand as she stepped across the gangplank. Without thinking she took it.

It was weird—she'd held his hand a thousand times before, and yet right now this one simple gesture was making her jittery, as though her whole body had been put on alert and was awaiting the next eager move.

Which was stupid. Ridiculous. And highly inconvenient.

Dammit, that was what came with sleeping with your bestie. Because now she couldn't stop the memories of those same hands roaming all over her body and doing things that had gotten her all hot and panting.

As they walked aft, she managed to surreptitiously slip her hand from his, avoiding his sideways glance by determinedly staring straight ahead.

God, she hated this awkwardness. They'd gone and done the unthinkable and ruined everything, and for a second, she felt that indescribable pain slice into her heart, leaving a deep and wounding scar in its wake. Things would never be the same again. It was like one of her disastrous relationships all over again, like everything her father had blurted out that one awful time in the heat of argument.

For God's sake, Kat, can you just for once not *be front-page news? Stop with all the attention and drama and just be a normal person?*

The shame burned briefly as she recalled his expression, a bitter twist of anger and disappointment. Then her thoughts were interrupted by the familiar hum and throb of engines as they entered the cabin.

She stopped in her tracks. "Are you casting off?"

"*Oui*. We're going to the island."

She gaped. Annoyance quickly morphed into fury. "Are you out of your mind? No!" She strode outside but it was too late. Furious, she whirled, pinning him with dagger eyes. "I didn't agree to this! And there's a cyclone on its way, in case you haven't noticed." She threw an arm wide, indicating the dock rapidly disappearing. "The town's in lockdown. *And* my car is at the marina."

He crossed his arms and leaned back onto the rail, then absently pushed back a curl as the wind whipped his hair around his face. "First, my house on the island is designed to withstand weather extremes, cyclones included. It's probably safer than most places on the mainland. Second, I'll call someone to pick up your car. And third, the reports say the island will only catch the edge of it—the eye will hit Cairns after 3:00 a.m."

"And by that time, we won't be able to return for God knows how long. No. Go back, Marco."

"No."

She growled. "I hate it when you get pushy."

His mouth quirked briefly but he said nothing. She continued to glare, putting all her anger into it, but he merely held her gaze calmly.

"You've been avoiding my calls," he finally said.

With a frustrated growl she whirled, planting her hands wide apart on the railing. "Dammit, you can be sooooo annoying!"

"Says the woman who *still* hasn't told me she's pregnant."

A moment passed, a moment in which Kat's heart sped up, then slowed down again as she closed her eyes and dropped her gaze to the churning black water below. A moment in which those meager rehearsed words all crumbled to ashes in her mouth, and she was left with nothing but the sound of slapping water and rushing air.

"I'm going to kill Connor."

Marco raised one dark eyebrow. "Don't blame him. He thought I should know."

Finally she straightened, crossed her arms and faced him. "Turn the boat around. It's not safe to be out."

"I checked with the coast guard. We're fine for at least another hour, enough time to get to the island." He shook his head. "And we have things to discuss."

"There's nothing to discuss."

A dark scowl bloomed. "You're kidding, right? You're *pregnant,* Kat. It's not just about you. It's about me, too."

She knew that. But the bubbling frustration inside forced the words from her mouth. "My body, my decision."

He stilled, his expression a mix of shock and seriousness. "Are you saying you want an abortion?"

She blinked, shaking her head as her stomach pitched in time with the waves. "Marco, you know what I went through with my mother. She was dead within two years of diagnosis. I could be a carrier."

He dragged a hand through his hair. "So get tested. I've been telling you that for years."

"I did. Plus, I do not have one single mothering bone in my body. Babies hate me and—"

"Whoa, whoa, whoa. Back up." He frowned and held up a hand. "You actually went and got *tested?*"

"Yes. Last week."

"After all these years of 'I don't want to know' and 'I don't want that hanging over my head, directing my choices in life'? All the times we argued when I tried to convince you otherwise?"

She nodded.

She'd shocked him, if his gaping expression was any indicator. "When were you going to tell me?" he finally bit out.

"I just did!" she snapped back, inwardly wincing at his thinly concealed hurt. "And speaking of not telling, what about you and Grace?"

"What about me and Grace?"

"So there *is* a you and Grace!"

He scowled, confused. "What the hell are you talking about?"

"You and her, having a baby together?"

From the look on his face, she'd stunned him. "Since when?"

"She told me you were back together."

He sighed, hands going to his hips. "Well, it's news to me. We've been over since before the *Coup de France*."

"How long before?"

"Way before our night together, *chérie*," he said softly.

She swallowed, refusing to allow herself a moment of remembrance. "So, you're saying Grace is lying?"

He shrugged. "Wishful thinking?"

She snapped her mouth shut, taking a deep, steady breath before mumbling, "This is a bloody disaster."

Was it her imagination, or did she see his mouth tighten? Then he sighed and dragged a hand through his hair and the moment was gone. "Kat, I can't stop you from making the final decision about what you do. If it were me, I'd be having the baby, regardless of those test results. But it's ultimately your choice."

"Then it's a good thing you're not me," she said quietly. "You weren't there. You didn't see what the disease did to my mother, every single day, for two years. I refuse to let that happen to my child."

His soft murmur sounded more like a groan. "Kat..."

The boat went over another wave, and suddenly the day's lunch didn't seem so secure in her stomach. She swallowed thickly then took a deep breath before meeting his eyes.

"I'll be here as much as you need me to be," he said, his gaze soft. "You're my best friend, *chérie,* and that's what friends do."

Friends. Her insides did another crazy swoop, just before the nausea surged again. This was no confession of love, no happily-ever-after, no I-can't-live-without-you. This was Marco offering his friendship and support, just as he'd always done throughout the tragedies of her embarrassingly public private life.

She swallowed a weird swell of abject disappointment. "Marco." She shook her head. "I don't know.... I haven't made any decision. Plus..." She took a breath. "I can't—I won't—have a baby just because you want it. And once this gets out—whatever my decision— there's going to be a media frenzy. Your career is more important than front-page gossip."

"Kat—"

"You know what the headlines were like last time. Do you honestly think I'd do that to you? I... Oh, God." She clutched her stomach.

He grabbed her arm, his face creased with alarm. "What's wrong? What—"

She turned to the railing but wasn't quick enough. In the next second, she threw up all over the deck, right on top of Marco's expensive Italian leather shoes.

Two

"Guess I should've seen that coming," Marco said drily as she rushed to the railing and continued to throw up over the side.

When he placed a gentle hand on her back, she shrugged it off with a groan. "Oh, God, don't."

His gaze darted from her to briefly stare up into the dark storm clouds. It was about to rain and rain hard, and if his captain, Larry, hurried, the crew could make it safely back to the mainland before it all came down. What he needed to discuss with Kat was between them alone; he certainly didn't need anyone else encroaching on their privacy.

He returned to Kat's doubled-up figure and shifted uncomfortably on the deck. He should've thought about seasickness. She wasn't a great sailor at the best of times, and with the added pregnancy, he wasn't surprised she'd thrown up.

"Can I get you anything?" he said now, frowning as her thick breath rattled in her throat. It tore little pieces from him, listening to her force down the nausea, willing herself not to throw up. She hated being sick, and he'd held her hair back on more than one occasion, watching helplessly as she went through the motions while he'd soothingly rubbed her back and made the appropriate sympathetic noises.

She stayed like that, bent over the railing, unfazed by the wind and ocean spray on her face until they finally docked at Sunset Island's small jetty twenty minutes later. As the boat edged slowly into position, Kat pulled herself upright, swiping at her mouth and swallowing thickly with a grimace.

"Bathroom," she muttered, and he silently watched her head into the cabin.

Five minutes later, as he was going over his choices in a long lineup of conversation starters, she emerged, her face pale and grim, a swipe of lip gloss on her mouth.

When she walked out onto the deck, that weird, tumultuous, out-of-control feeling had receded, only to be replaced with trepidation. This crazy situation was totally out of his hands, and that thought freaked the hell out of him. Yet she…she looked so cool and blank as she strode toward him that he felt the sudden urge to kiss her, to dislodge that perfect composure and make her as frustrated and confused as he felt.

Stupid idea. Because Kat had made it clear she wanted to forget what they'd done all those weeks ago. And if he looked at this logically, that was the sensible thing to do. They were best friends. Throughout all their sucky personal relationships, her mother's death, his one marriage and divorce, her two, plus the crazy media attention they always seemed to attract, their friendship endured. Sure, the papers always hinted at something more, but they'd both laughed and shrugged it off a long time ago.

Yet now, as his insides pitched with uncharacteristic uncertainty, she looked almost…calm. As if she'd already made a decision and was confident in making it.

She was so damn strong. Sometimes too strong. Just one of the things that both attracted and annoyed him.

"I don't know what more we have to discuss," she said now, watching his crew prepare to dock. "This is a waste of time. Plus, with the approaching cyclone, we need to let people know where we are."

"I called the authorities before we left, plus your father, my mother and Connor," he said calmly.

"Wow. You really planned ahead for this, didn't you?"

He ignored her sarcasm. "All bases are covered. We're perfectly safe."

Her face creased with such serious doubt that he had to smother a laugh.

Safe? No way, not when her expression became suddenly tight and he knew exactly where her thoughts were going. If they were anything like his, it was back to That Night, replaying every intimate second over and over, despite his determination to shove it to the back of his mind. She didn't want to be stuck anywhere with him, least of all in such an intimate personal space.

Her breath snapped in, eyes darkening just before she glanced away, and his groin tightened. It was incredibly arousing, knowing she was obviously remembering their crazy-hot lovemaking. Lovemaking that had, instead of quenching the hunger, only succeeded in stoking his desire for more.

His low groan was lost in the noisy preparations for docking, yet when he gently took her arm, she shot him a dark scowl and dug her heels in.

His eyebrows ratcheted up. "You're going to stay on the boat in protest?"

"I should."

"Well, that's a dumb idea. A storm's coming, in case you hadn't noticed."

"You're the one who dragged me out here."

He sighed. "Look, *chérie,* come to the house. If you want to yell at me, at least we'll be safe."

She paused, seeming to go through her limited options, until her chin went up and she shot him a glare. "Fine. But as soon as the storm's passed, you're taking me home."

He almost smiled. Almost. "Okay."

She gave him a final look then swept past him, down the gangplank and onto the rickety jetty, her heels echoing dully as he commanded his crew to take the spare vessel and return to the mainland.

They took a golf buggy to the house, efficiently moving along the road that edged the west side of Sunset Island. Just like all the times before, when the place came into sight, Kat held her breath and marveled at the architecture of the magnificent six-bedroom house. It was all glass and timber walls set in a lush tropical rain forest, with natural lines, arches and a sloping roof set on sturdy stilts, perfectly sheltered among the vegetation to avoid the fiercest storms yet taking spectacular advantage of the amazing Pacific Ocean sunsets.

This was Marco's haven, a place he could relax and be himself with his friends. The guy she knew so very well. The guy who was now intimate with her body, who had made her moan and climax.

As Kat ran her eyes over the house's familiar lines and tried not to think about *that,* the buggy wound its way along the driveway, until finally they stopped at the front door and Marco got out. Again, he offered his hand and she was forced to take it, although she quickly released him as soon as she stepped out.

"We need to secure the shutters before the storm hits," he said, eyeing the sky.

Kat nodded and followed him to the long path edged with a sturdy safety railing that ran all the way around the house. As the wind slowly picked up and the trees began to sway, they both worked in silence, cranking down the storm shutters covering the multitude of windows. With the last one firmly in place, they returned to the front.

"The birds and the bats flew off a few hours ago," Marco commented, frowning into the dark sky. "They know something's wrong."

A chill ran over her skin. "The Bureau of Meteorology said the main eye is bound for Cairns."

"Yeah, they're bracing for the worst—mobile phone towers down, power outages. The ports will be closed, too. So, not the best place to be right now. Let's get inside."

"I've got nothing to wear," she said suddenly as she stepped in the door.

"You've still got some stuff from last time. And you can borrow from me if you need to."

Walking around in Marco's clothes, smelling his scent, knowing the exact same garments had been right up next to his skin? Just. No.

Kat said nothing as she walked into the familiar coolness of the slate foyer, down the hall to the back of the house, past the amazing indoor pool with wet bar to her right, the elegant water feature bubbling away to her left.

Finally she reached the heart of the house—the huge combined kitchen and entertainment area with comfy sofas, a wide-screen plasma TV, dining table to the side, curved walls with floor-to-ceiling windows and a fully equipped kitchen. She and his guests always spent their time here, eating and talking current affairs, the state of the world, his second home in Marseille and the ever-present topic, European football.

She went straight to the fridge, grabbed a ginger beer and then walked to the barricaded windows that normally displayed an uninterrupted one-eighty view of the Pacific Ocean.

During the day the simple beauty of searing blue sky stretched forever until it eventually dipped to kiss the dark ocean in the far distance. At night, the absolute blackness enveloped everything, the only respite the tiny mainland lights on the horizon. Except this time she was more than acutely aware of the brewing storm playing out behind the shutters, matching her churning thoughts as she heard Marco's firm footfalls on the polished marble behind her. The vague scent of his aftershave brought back the uncomfortable memories from that one night, ten weeks ago.

"So we should be clear of the storm here," she began, her back still to him, the cold ginger-beer bottle cradled against her warm neckline.

"Yes." He reached for the patio door handle and swung it wide, walking out onto the lit deck. "But we've still got a warning and need to take all precautions."

"Your cellar," she said as he began to collect the deck chairs.

He nodded then grinned. "And you guys teased me for converting it."

She pulled a chair inside the back door. "Well, to be fair, the worst you'd ever seen was a tropical rainstorm, not a cyclone."

"Always a first time for everything."

Those words took on a whole new meaning tonight. She watched him carry the patio chairs inside, waiting for him to break the silence as she picked at the label on her ginger-beer bottle.

He finally closed and locked the door, and after a few minutes of him shoving the chairs into a corner and saying nothing, she was about ready to break.

"Marco—"

"Kat—"

They both turned and spoke at the same time, but it was Kat who paused for him to continue. When he sighed and ran a hand through his hair, she wanted to groan out loud. She knew exactly what that hair felt like in her fingers, how soft it was, how it curled and waved with a life of its own, and how with one gentle tug at the nape she could direct his mouth to a better place on her neck....

Oh, God, I have to stop thinking about that!

When she glanced up, he was looking at her with

those dark eyes, assessing her every word, movement and expression until she felt vaguely underdressed. Ridiculous, because the last thing on his mind right now was getting her naked and into bed.

What a vision that conjured up. *No. No! Stop it!*

Then he abruptly turned and the moment shattered.

"You need food," he said, striding over to the kitchen and opening the fridge door. "And we need to prepare for tonight."

Her stomach took that moment to remind her of her long-gone lunch, and with a sigh she followed him over, her mind on the immediate problem of her empty belly. "What do you have?"

He waved his hand inside the fridge. "You choose. I'm going to tape up the windows."

Kat prepared bread rolls, cheese, cold meats and potato salad while Marco placed thick tape across all the windows. After they ate, they sat on the sofa and had coffee, the muted TV spurting out nonstop cyclone updates.

It was a familiar scenario—the coffee, the silent television, their seating positions: she at one corner, sprawled across two spots and hugging a pillow, he in the opposite corner with ankles and arms crossed. Yet the unspoken tension in the air was smoke-thick and just as hard to ignore.

This time it was Kat who broke the silence. "You know, Grace was arranging a surprise dinner for your return."

His eyebrow went up. "Was she?"

"Yeah."

"Right." The slight grimace in his expression spoke volumes.

"What's that look for?"

"What look?"

"Don't give me that. You know the one."

He sighed. "I don't know why she keeps bothering. We broke up months ago."

"I see," Kat said slowly, pressing her lips together. Marco would never lie to her—so *was* it all wishful thinking on Grace's part? She frowned. Yeah, Grace liked to talk up all her relationships—that TV exec three months ago, the Russian writer, the ex-soapie star.

Then Marco abruptly turned on the couch, giving her his full attention, and she forgot all about Grace's love life.

"Kat, this is me here. We talk about pretty much everything—"

"Not *everything*."

He gave her a look. "Just stop avoiding the issue and talk to me now. Let's think this baby situation over logically."

She shook her head. "Were you not listening about the tests?"

"I didn't ask that. I asked if you wanted to have this baby."

"I am *not* turning this discussion into a pro-choice debate."

He scowled. "I'm not trying to. All I'm asking is for you to consider all your options."

Her insides ached. "That's *all* I've been doing since I found out. Marco, please don't do this. I can't get attached, knowing there's a possibility it will be carrying a fatal disease. Plus, I know women are supposed to have these ticking body clocks, supposed to be filled with a great burning need to be mothers, but I am telling you, I'm not one of them."

And yet…there'd been a few moments where she'd allowed her imagination to drift, where her thoughts had been occupied by something other than work, her swish Cairns apartment and all those solitary nights stretching before her. She'd imagined an unfamiliar future consisting of a house, a garden, a husband and babies. A scary, scary thought that had her breath catching and her heart racing every time she let her mind wander there.

No.

She sighed. "I…I don't know what to say. I really don't."

"Well, that's a start. At least it means you're not wedded to the idea of an abortion."

"I'm not making any decision until the tests come back. I'm not going to…" She swallowed and glanced away. "Not going to get attached to the idea if they come back positive. And anyway, what on earth am I going to do with a baby? This is *me* we're talking about here."

His scowl deepened. "Don't be ridiculous. You're a great person. You're funny and gorgeous and smart, and you have people in your life who love you."

She flushed under the unexpected praise. "But a *mother?*"

"Other women begin with a whole lot less."

"But it's a full-time job. A lifelong commitment." She worried the edge of the pillow, picking at the stitching. "You can't get a do-over with these things. What if I stuff it up?"

"Nobody's perfect at parenting—just look at Connor's family. I guarantee you'd do a lot better than them."

Kat nodded. It was impossible to avoid the Blairs, especially when her father and Connor's were business partners at Jackson & Blair. Unlike her relationship with Marco's parents, she'd never warmed to Stephen Blair, a ruthlessly ambitious man with a penchant for blondes, and his wife, Corinne, a cold gym-junkie socialite with a Botox habit. Connor's childhood was a perfect study in fractured family dynamics. A therapist's dream… more so than her own.

"My dad isn't much better," she said now. "He'd rather hold a grudge about old headlines than dole out any praise."

"At least they were happy, well, until…" He trailed off diplomatically.

Until her mother's diagnosis. Kat silently filled in the sentence. They had been strict but fair, even when she'd stretched the limits with the usual teenage smoking, drinking and sneaking out to parties. Certainly not overly demonstrative in their affections. But after her mother's diagnosis, her father had turned into an angry, bitter man, always judgmental, always unhappy. And Kat could never do anything right, from her decision to drop out of Brisbane University to her crazy, wild nights on the town that were her one respite from thinking about her mother's disease.

Until one particular night when she'd stumbled home at sunrise in a highly drunken state and her father had been waiting for her, scorn pouring from every tense muscle.

"You've had everything we could give you, and look

at you! Your mother is dying, so you throw in a perfectly good education to get drunk every weekend!"

"Maybe that's the point!" she'd stormed back. *"It's in my head every single waking moment. I need some time to clear it out, to just forget, otherwise I'll go crazy!"*

His fists had clenched, and for one awful moment she'd wondered whether he'd give in to the temptation and actually hit her. Instead he'd cut her with words, his particular specialty.

A month later her mother had died and Kat had run away to France, where Marco was the current darling of French football. Where she'd slowly come to realize there was more to her tiny little world than short skirts, wild parties and free drinks.

Kat swallowed, pushing the memory aside. God, no wonder the press had loved to hate her. She'd been such a spoiled little rich girl.

"But you've grown since then," Marco said now. "And he's still stuck in the past, rehashing old arguments. We don't have to be our parents. Not with our child."

Our child. Those two words were like a blow to the chest, leaving a shallow breath rattling in her throat.

"Look, Marco, let's be honest. You've worked incredibly hard to get where you are. You've got a great career and an amazing, wonderful life. No commitment, no ties—"

"Kat…"

"No, let me finish. You can jump on a plane at a moment's notice and be on the other side of the world. You have your pick of women—and there are a *lot* of women."

"Kat—"

She ignored the warning growl in his voice and kept going. "I'm not going to force you to change, and a baby does that, in ways you can't even imagine. The media frenzy will affect both our lives and careers."

"If you choose to keep the baby, then I'll do the right thing."

She blinked. "The right thing? What, are we living in the 1950s now? You don't have to marry me because I'm pregnant."

He paused, a second too long. "Who said anything about marriage? I'm talking about being here for you. As your friend."

She frowned, the unexpected sliver of disappointment stabbing hard. Oh, so now she wasn't good enough to marry, was that it? But just as she was about to open her mouth and say exactly that, she snapped it shut. That was manipulation of the worst kind, and she refused to do it. She couldn't put Marco in that position—she wouldn't. And marriage was the last thing she wanted.

"Good thing, too. I suck at relationships," she said lightly, her hand tight on the coffee cup. "I've tried too many times, but I just don't have that particular gene. They're messy, they're painful and they always end in disaster. I don't want to ruin our friendship."

"You don't suck. You didn't force James to cheat. You didn't hand the press those photos." Marco's brows took a dive, his expression dark. "And as for Ben…"

"Please do *not* remind me." If there was a Disastrous Relationship Museum, hers would take front and center as prime exhibit number one: her first marriage to Jackson & Blair's publicity manager, Ben Freeman, when she was twenty-two. He'd turned out to be a selfish, misogynistic bastard. Her second marriage five years later, a quickie Bali wedding to Marco's teammate, annulled after just seventy-two hours when she'd caught James screwing a waitress in their bridal suite. And then her engagement to Aussie Rules' wild child Ezio Cantoni barely a year ago. *He'd* taken nude shower shots of her then "accidentally" leaked them to the tabloids.

She was done with the scrutiny, the uncertainty, the angst. It was painful and humiliating and downright tiring. For her sanity and self-respect, it was just not worth the effort. And now she was bringing a child into that?

Kat sighed, shifting on the sofa. "And honestly, Marco, how are you going to be involved? Weren't you planning to move back to France after the Football Federation of Australia's awards in three weeks?"

"That was one option."

Her brow ratcheted up. "That's not how you talked about it a few months ago."

He sighed and cast an eye to the shuttered window. "I've got a lot of things going on—the coaching clinics, the sponsorship stuff. Plus my network contract is up for renegotiation next month. I haven't decided about France yet."

She paused for long, drawn-out seconds. "Oh, no. Don't you *dare* start to rethink anything. I won't allow it."

"You won't allow it?"

"No." She ignored his irritation with a wave of her hand. "We're not married. Hell, we're not even a couple. Just…best friends who may be having a baby."

He said nothing, just looked toward the shuttered windows and then the wall clock that read quarter past one. "It sounds to be getting worse outside." He stood. "We should go downstairs."

She paused, glancing toward the windows, then nodded. "Okay."

He offered his hand and she automatically took it, the sudden urgency of the moment pushing their discussion into the background. The innocent warmth of his fingers wrapped around hers created a frustratingly intimate sensation that she was loath to give up. He took her down the hall, to a door that led to the basement and his wine cellar, which he'd modified with this kind of situation in mind.

The wine was stacked neatly to the left of the small room, and to the right sat a couch, a fixed, fully stocked bar fridge and a small generator that powered the soft lamps that were now lit in preparation.

She hesitated at the door, scanning the room as reality flooded in.

"Don't worry, *chérie,*" Marco said beside her, giving her fingers a reassuring squeeze. "We're perfectly safe."

Again, that word. The door was heavy but he closed it with ease, and when he turned to her, she swallowed the panic and offered a shaky smile.

They settled quickly in the room, Kat automatically going over to prepare coffee, Marco checking the small ventilation window high on the far wall and then the lights. After a few more minutes, they sat on the couch, Marco pulled out a pack of UNO cards and they settled in for the night.

"So how's working for Grace going? Still a pain in the butt?" Marco asked casually as he shuffled the pack.

"Oh, she's not that bad."

"Hmm." His expression was skeptical as he dealt them seven cards apiece.

She sighed. "Actually, I miss my old London job."

"What, the one you took up between Ben and James?"

"Ugh." She made a face. "My life's most significant moments reduced to a 'between exes' reference."

"Sorry." Marco's expression looked anything but. "Let me rephrase. The Oxfam job you took at the age of twenty-five when you spent a couple of years living and working in London in blissful anonymity."

She gave him a look, not entirely convinced he wasn't being sarcastic, before finally nodding. "It was only a year, but I felt better about that job than anything I've ever done. I felt like I should—" She cut herself off abruptly, her thumbnail going to her mouth, teeth worrying it.

"Like you should what?" He picked up his cards and fanned them expertly.

"Like I should do something more. Donate to charity or start up a foundation or something."

She waited for him to voice doubt, to echo her father's familiar refrain about giving up a perfectly good job for an uncertain dream when she'd casually mentioned the subject a few months ago. Instead he just looked at her and said, "You've never mentioned that before."

She shrugged and overturned the first card on the top of the deck. "I stopped thinking about it after I told my dad."

"Let me guess—he said you don't know a thing about running a charity, it's too expensive, why chuck in a perfectly stable job for a dubious flight of fancy in this economy when you'll lose interest in the first year?"

"All of the above."

He sighed and placed a yellow two on the pile. The

sudden silence sat heavy in the air now, until Marco finally spoke. "Have you done the figures? Worked out how much it would take to do something like that?"

"No."

"So work it out. Make a business plan. Talk to your old workmates. Call your accountant. Screw your father. I mean that in the nicest possible way," he added with a thin smile and placed the first card down on the table. "You're smart and clever and you have experience. You can work a crowd, raise funds and know how to handle the press. Whatever happens with those tests and the baby, you can still do this."

She stared at her hand, rearranging the cards by color as her mind worked furiously. Oh, she wanted to. In between the many fluff pieces and gossip segments *Morning Grace* aired, the human-interest stories drew her the most. The burning compulsion to do something herself, to help ease someone's burden, to bring a little joy into the lives of people who really needed it, got her every time. She always ended up donating to every cause she sourced. Every time.

"This'll be bigger than a ten-minute segment," Marco said now. "You'll be able to give things more media coverage, follow it through, devote more time. Really make a difference."

She put a Draw Two on the pile and murmured something noncommittal, signaling the end of the discussion.

Marco said no more and for the next half hour they played cards and pretended everything was fine, even though the faint sounds of the creaking house and the wind as it picked up forced their attention from the game a dozen times. Finally Marco turned on the small radio and the room was filled with a steady stream of weather updates.

When the lights suddenly went out, Kat jumped. Yet when the generator kicked in seconds later and the lights clicked back on, it did nothing to assuage her growing panic.

"What are we even doing here?" she muttered, flicking her thumb along the edge of her cards, eyeing the lights, then the generator. "We went out in a cyclone warning, for God's sake! This is stupid, not to mention dangerous."

"We're not in its direct path. Would I honestly do something to put us in danger? Trust me. We're safe."

When she shivered, he handed her the blanket from the couch, draping it around her shoulders, tucking it close. She half expected a tender forehead kiss to finish. Damn, she was actually wishing for it. He'd kissed her before, an I-love-you-you're-my-best-friend kiss on the cheek or the forehead. And they'd hugged more frequently than she could count. But tellingly, he'd never kissed her on the lips. Until That Night.

For the next twenty minutes they kept playing cards as the rain and howling wind picked up, the updates morphing into location reports and interviews of people in organized shelters and those who chose to stay in their homes and see the storm through.

Half an hour later, it hit.

Card game now forgotten, they sat in tense silence, hip to knee on the couch, glued to the radio. The wind screamed past the house, ripping through the trees and banging the shutters in their frames. From inside their refuge, they could hear the rush of air, the snap and crack of trees bending and breaking under the raw elements, debris being thrown around. The house remained firm but the wind and slashing rain was a constant, picking up in waves then petering out until the minutes stretched like hours.

The radio spat out crucial information as the cyclone careened across the coast, and as time crawled into an hour, then two, and the cyclone finally passed through Cairns and headed south before dying down a few miles out to sea, details began to trickle in. Details of devastating damage, heart-wrenchingly revealed via the mainland survivors.

"We're gonna have to start over. We've lost everything."

"We have family, friends, community. We'll survive this."

"I don't know whether we can rebuild. We weren't insured."

"Well, you just pick up and move on, don't you? You just get it done."

"Please, help us. Our house…everything. It's gone. We need help."

Kat's breath caught, the sob forming low in her throat as she listened to that last one, a woman and her family who'd been right in the storm's path. It ripped at her like claws, and she unashamedly let silent tears well as the extent of the damage was slowly and thoroughly detailed over the course of an hour.

When Marco's hand went to her knee, patting reassuringly, she jumped, eyes flying to his.

The look on his face undid her, a mix of sorrow and understanding that reflected everything she'd tried to keep inside. She watched him swallow, her gaze fol-

lowing his thumb as he leaned in to gently wipe away
her tears.

"Don't cry," he said softly, knuckles and thumb resting firmly on her cheekbone. "It's okay."

Her breath jagged. "But all those people…"

"They'll rebuild. You know that. No fatalities have
been reported, so that's one good thing. It'll be okay.
We're safe."

She sniffed, unable to look away from his concerned
gaze. "I was scared."

"I know." He cupped her face and leaned in, placing
his warm mouth first on one cheek, then the other. Years
ago, the familiar French-style greeting had amused her.
But now, with his lips so very close to hers, and then
as she watched him slowly pull back with a soft smile
creasing those dreamy eyes, her heart leaped.

*Keep calm, Kat. If you stop acting normal around
him, he'll know something is wrong.* But could she honestly do all those little things, the smiling, the hugs, the
casual touching, and not be affected by what they'd
done?

Her gaze darted to that mouth, that lovely, lush
mouth that seemed like an evil conspiracy on a man
already so beautiful.

Yes, *beautiful* was the only word to describe Marco
Corelli. Outwardly he appeared cocky and confident,
working the crowd, the camera, the press with smooth
ease that trod a fine line between charming and practiced. He always got what he wanted, be it an interview,
a prime restaurant table or a woman. But she also knew
him better than anyone else and knew that public persona was only a small part of what made him tick. He

was generous. Fiercely loyal. Fiery and passionate about the things and people he loved.

She could feel his eyes on her, taking in her expression, every single movement, and it was then that she realized she'd been staring at his mouth and daydreaming like some mooning soccer groupie.

With a suddenly dry throat, she darted her gaze to his.

And her breath stuttered all over again.

Three

Kat didn't know what happened because it was instantaneous, although in reality it probably took a little longer than that. All she knew was one second she was sitting there, heart pounding, his hand still cupping her face, the imprint of his warm mouth on her skin. Then his gaze slipped to her lips, she parted them, he made some choked sound and suddenly he swooped down and they were kissing.

Her arms went around his neck as if they belonged there. She groaned, opened up for him and was gone.

He dragged her to his chest, cradling her, almost as if inviting her to sink into him. So she did.

During the long, hot, unbelievable kiss, she felt his hands everywhere, tugging her clothing, sweeping over her skin, caressing and touching until she was all heated up and her heart throbbed hard against her ribs. Then he pushed her back, bunching her skirt around her waist, and she was grabbing his shirt, yanking it from his pants and fumbling with the waistband.

"Let me." He pushed her hands aside, quickly dragging down his pants, his urgency fueling her arousal as her mouth locked on his. Her blood raced as he jammed a knee between her legs, pushing them roughly apart then settling his hips against her before suddenly and swiftly entering her.

A harsh breath hissed from her lips, matching his as she stared into those dark eyes that bled black with passion, and she nearly lost it then and there. Then he uttered a low growl, hitched her leg around his waist, pinned her hands above her head and started to move.

She couldn't think, couldn't breathe, from the raw, animal sensation of being filled, fully and completely. He wasn't tender or slow. He didn't offer romantic words of love. He simply took, and when she got over the shock of the moment, she took, too, welcoming him, grinding her hips hard into his, her breath rushing out in a harsh groan, her teeth nipping the sensitive spot where his neck met shoulder. He cursed softly when she did that, upping the pace so she slammed into the sofa, the cushions grazing her skin. She gasped but kept moving, knowing full well she'd have wool burns come morning but totally beyond caring. Instead the moment took her, wiped away any reality until it was just them, their harsh breath coupling in the eerie silence and the air full of the familiar scent of sex and need.

Breathless and throbbing, she impatiently rocked her hips against his, eager for the final release. And when her climax came, it rushed in with little warning, and she was left floundering as the waves crashed, leaving her shaking and panting. Dimly she was aware that Marco still had her hands pinned, his deep murmur of release against her lips as he followed her, his body jerking into hers. She shook, his satisfaction heightening hers, and she tightened her leg around his waist, cradling his body, taking all of him with a groan that ripped from deep inside.

It was…he was… She groaned again and closed her eyes, willing reality to stay away for just a moment more so she could just enjoy this, them, here and now.

But of course, it wasn't possible. Reality always intruded.

The air cooled her naked flesh. His breath on her neck slowed. The shudders racking her body subsided. And soon, the angry wind against the house broke into their private moment. When he gently released her hands, blood rushed into her fingers once more. And slowly, so very slowly, she felt him slip from her body and then stand.

They'd done it again. After everything she'd told herself, every warning she'd mentally listed.

She opened her mouth to say something, closed it and then opened it again before giving up. Instead she sat up, yanked her skirt down and began to button up in the embarrassing silence, pointedly ignoring Marco as he did the same.

But when they were done and literally had nothing else to distract them, Kat sighed and finally looked up.

Marco had moved to the far end of the couch and was packing up their card game.

"Marco…" she began, her throat dry.

"Hmm?"

"I… We…" She paused, hands going to her lap as he continued to tidy. "Can you stop that and look at me?"

When he paused and finally met her gaze, she had to bite back a soft groan. He looked so serious, the raw curves of his face drawn into such a solemn expression that she was sorely tempted to trace her finger down his cheek to coax a smile from his full lips.

Lovely lips that she'd had the thorough pleasure of just moments before.

"What on earth are we doing?" she said now, acutely aware of the warm flush heating her skin. "How did we get to this?"

With a sigh, he flopped into the chair and crossed an ankle over one knee. "Well, the first time, alcohol was involved."

"And this time there's…" She waved a hand, indicating the storm outside that had eased into a dull rumble. "But that's not what I meant. I've never…thought of you in *that* way before."

"I see."

She couldn't meet his eyes without getting embarrassed, and that realization just flustered her further. Truth was, she'd thought about it more than once but every time refused to indulge for more than a few moments. Giving the fantasy more than that would've been weird, not to mention futile. He'd never seen her as more than a best friend, so what was the point? She'd been content with the tag for all those years.

Until now, apparently.

Dammit. She felt her entire body warm under his scrutiny, until the desperate need to move overwhelmed her. So she rose, went to the small bar fridge and fished out a bottle of water. With her back to him, she rolled the bottle over her neck then down, welcoming the icy shock on her hot skin.

She was exhausted, so tired of thinking. She had no idea where she stood. Her head was a mess, and she couldn't even blame this lapse on alcohol as she had last time.

The heat of the moment? Yeah, nah. She could have stopped if she'd really wanted to. She just didn't want to. She *wanted* to taste his mouth, have his body slide over hers. Wanted to feel his hot breath on her skin and have him fill her in the most primitive way possible.

He made her forget things, just for a while.

She twisted off the bottle cap and took a slow swig, her thoughts churning. She shouldn't be distracted, not now. She had other things to consider, important, life-changing events.

Swallowing the water, she stared at the small ventilation window that would herald a new morning, full of light and promise. A brand-new morning revealing the wild chaos of a passing cyclone. As the radio had revealed these past few hours, so many people had lost everything, and not only their homes. Personal effects, memories, things that meant so much to them, had been swept away by Mother Nature in the space of a few hours. It really was a miracle no one had died.

Relief surged, shaking her for one second before she swiftly got a handle on it. She was alive. So was Marco. They'd eventually return to the mainland, check over any damage to their homes, and she'd get the results of her test then make an informed decision based on those results.

Belatedly, she realized Grace would want her on the cyclone coverage, would need her expert digging to find that unique special-interest story that would spearhead the show's donation line. They'd done it for the Queensland floods, for the bushfires, even New Zealand's recent earthquake. Yet as she stood there with the cyclone's aftereffects thinning outside, punctuated by the constant radio chatter, all she could think about was…

Her test results.

Marco. A baby.

Their *baby*.

And her thoughts scrambled once more, rendering speech useless.

Marco kept his gaze firmly on her as she pointedly ignored his scrutiny. Her warm brown hair was sexily tousled, her neck flushed with faint stubble burn and the buttons on her shirt were crooked where she'd hastily tried to gather her composure.

"I guess," he finally said in answer to her previous question, "that we're giving in to some latent sexual tension, which is only heightened by the storm outside."

Startled, she flicked him a glance as she took another drink. "Sure."

He waited for more but she remained silent, all her attention firmly on her water bottle.

So of course, his eyes wandered, lingering on those long legs, the dip of her waist. The almost nonexistent curve of her stomach.

And suddenly an overwhelming bolt of emotion shot through him, a mixture of desire and fierce protection for both her and that unbelievable spark of life growing in her belly. No one except a handful of people knew the real Kat—the loving, fun woman who'd do anything for a friend, who'd wrestled with her parents' overprotective influence her entire life. Who'd been dragged through her own personal hell thanks to her mother's illness, front-page headlines and a bunch of loser men who frankly didn't deserve her.

She was intelligent, passionate…and stubborn. Way too stubborn. Once she made her mind up about something, there was no way she'd change it back.

Like that damn stupid decision not to get tested. It twisted like a splinter in his gut every time he allowed himself to think about it, every time he tried to convince her to just go and find out. And now she'd finally done it.

Even though she was avoiding his eyes, he knew she knew he was staring. The tension in her shoulders, the way her mouth tightened, all gave her away. And stubbornly he kept on staring.

After half a minute's standoff, he gave up and turned up the radio. Eventually she came over and sat in the chair opposite and they listened in silence, the weather updates and on-location reporters slowly charging the air with a sense of growing concern.

Finally she said, "Is it…? Do you…feel weird?"

He glanced up, but her eyes remained firmly on the radio. "What? The cyclone?"

"No, us."

He felt many things, but weird wasn't one of them. "No, actually. You?"

"Yes. No." Her gaze darted to a spot past his shoulder before returning to the radio. "I…don't know."

"Okay."

She sighed, her elbows on the table, her thumbnail going automatically to her mouth before she stopped halfway and dropped her hand. "This is…" She finally shook her head. "It's… We shouldn't have done this."

"A bit late now, *chérie*." He swallowed the small blow she dealt with no outward sign. "Although I totally expected that response."

Her eyes snapped to his. "Did you?"

"Mmm. You have a tendency to run when things get too…intimate."

"I do not!"

He lifted one eyebrow at her outrage. "You do."

Her eyes narrowed as she leaned back in the chair and slowly crossed her arms. "Ben was a selfish bastard who dumped me when he realized I was serious about not wanting kids."

"I wasn't talking about *him*." His hands involuntarily clenched at the memory. "And I still think you should've let me deck him."

"And have you charged with assault? No way."

He shook his head. "Anyway, I'm talking metaphorically as well as physically."

"James was screwing a woman in our hotel room. Ezio took naked photos of me and sold them to a gossip mag." She shoved a stray strand of hair back off her shoulder. "These are all deal breakers for me."

"And what about us, Kat? Is best-friend sex one of your deal breakers?"

"Sex *always* ruins things."

He frowned at her too-quick answer. Again, she was dancing around the question. But when she glanced away, hiding her expression from view in an uncharacteristically shy move, man, the sudden desire to kiss her pulled low and tight in his gut. Instead he swallowed the urge and remained where he was.

"So what are we going to do now?" he asked, deliberately casual.

She shrugged. "The media—"

"Screw the media," he growled, putting both palms flat on the table. "What do *you* want to do?"

"Marco…" His name came out as a groan, her fingers going to her temple, where she rubbed firmly. "I'm tired. I know it's your thing to talk things over ad nauseum, but can we just not right now? Please?"

He took in how she was reclining in the chair, her half-lidded eyes, the creases bracketing her mouth, and a sliver of guilt shot through his gut. "You should really get some sleep."

For once, she didn't argue. "So should you."

He shrugged. "I'm still on European time. Not that tired. Here." He stood and rearranged the pillows. "Sleep."

After a second's hesitation, she went to the couch and sat, then stretched out. He quickly dragged the blanket up over her.

"Thanks," she muttered, her eyes heavy as he covered her feet.

He moved to the single armchair and had just settled into it as her eyes closed. Moments later, her breath slowed and she was asleep.

With a small smile he got comfy, crossed his arms and ankles and let his mind drift.

He swept his gaze over her, from the dark lashes resting on the soft curve of her cheek and the soft hair streaming down her neck, to her long, lean body, which took up the entire couch. They'd been friends forever, ever since that embarrassing moment in Year Nine had changed everything. Fourteen was such a cocky, self-

indulgent age, and he'd been the worst, so full of attitude and mouth. He'd made a stupid comment, showing
off to his friends, and Kat had surprisingly struck back,
shoving him so hard he'd fallen on his ass. He'd jok-
ingly admitted that had been the start of his adoration,
and their combined detention plus her innocent smile,
offbeat humor and fierce loyalty had only cemented
their relationship.

From then on they'd been a tight quartet—him, Luke,
Connor and Kat—until he'd been offered the unbelievable opportunity to play European football and left
Australia for France when he was sixteen. Then their
individual lives had taken over—him with his soccer
career, her with her mother's illness and her various tabloid exploits. He'd been shocked to see her three years
later, barely a month after her mother's death, but he'd
never questioned it, instead taking up right where they'd
left their friendship. They'd traveled, she'd crashed at
his house in Marseille for a few months and from there
she'd bounced between Europe and Sydney for close to
six years. It was like she'd been trying to find her place
in the world, and until her stint in London, he wasn't
sure she'd find it. But then, three years ago, she'd landed
the *Morning Grace* job, and since then, she'd actually
been happy. Sure, they'd both had relationship woes
and she'd been his shoulder through the excruciating
years his father had been dragged through the press,
then an inquiry, before finally being cleared of money-
laundering charges last year. She'd been his go-to girl
when he'd been in between girlfriends and needed a
date for some function or event. She was his wingman.
His best friend. And now his lover.

She was having a baby. His baby. Theirs.

He swallowed thickly, a dozen emotions churning as he imagined her—his Kat—growing big with their child. Glowing, smiling. Happy.

But she isn't, is she?

His brows took a dive. *Don't think about that.*

For once, she wasn't talking. Odd, because they'd never had any problems talking about any topic, from exes to family to everything in between.

Well, almost everything. The ban on relationship talk was still in force, even though he'd wanted to overstep that boundary dozens of times. But for her, he'd bitten his lip and stayed frustratingly silent.

His speculative gaze ran over her sleeping form again. She might project a haughty, almost cool confidence to the world now, but to her closest friends she was just Kat Jackson, filled with doubt, frustration and a dozen dreams she worried she'd miss out on. She had a wicked sense of humor. She read literary fiction as well as popular crime novels. She was a *Star Wars* fanatic but adored the *Star Trek* reboots, had an insane collection of anime art and eighties retro music. She hated pickles on her burger, loved penguins and handbags, was funny, gorgeous, impatient, argumentative and incredibly intelligent.

And yet the press had first tagged her as ditzy and shallow, a party girl of the craziest kind with a penchant for bad boys. It didn't help that she'd gone overboard when she'd turned seventeen, bouncing from one publicity event to the next, dressed in designer heels and revealing clothing, getting snapped drunk by every single reporter eager to plaster Keith Jackson's spoiled baby girl all over the gossip pages. Not surprising that she'd taken up a position as society reporter, a job that had lasted until her mother's death.

He'd been living in France, where he'd quickly become Marseille's *Ligue 1* star forward on a million-dollar contract, treated like a rock star wherever he went. Ridiculous really, for a kid barely out of his teens to be suddenly thrust into celebrity life, rubbing shoulders with the rich and famous, dating supermodels and actresses, all while his best friend had been wrestling with life-changing events.

A low growl forced itself through clenched teeth before he bit it back. She'd turned up on his doorstep a week after Marseille had won the *Coupe de France* and broken down in his arms. Then they'd spent three months during his off-season backpacking through Europe, clearing their heads and getting their friendship back on track.

Those months had been a wake-up call for him, too. He'd stopped drinking, started making responsible choices, investing his money instead of blowing it all on thousand-dollar bottles of champagne, designer jewelry he'd never wear and vintage cars he'd never drive. And it had also been a turning point in their friendship. Now they were both thirty-three and had never gone longer than two days without a call or a text, except when he was traveling on business. And they told each other everything, no matter how private or painful. Well, except for that no-go relationship zone.

He still couldn't believe she'd actually gone and gotten tested. God, he still remembered that huge argument, a week after her mother's death, when they'd nearly ruined their friendship for good.

"How can you not want to know?" he'd demanded.

"Because I don't! I don't want a death sentence affecting how I live my life!"

She wasn't alone in thinking that, either. He'd done the research. He knew more people chose to remain in the dark about being a fatal-disease carrier. Yet it still didn't stop his heart from contracting every time he thought of her, his Kat, suffering the same fate as her mother. Dead within two years of diagnosis.

Marco released a long, slow breath, his eyes darting to the ventilation window at the far end of the cellar. The wind had downgraded to a strong breeze, the low hum of radio chatter white noise against it all. He grabbed a bottle of water and unscrewed the top, downing the contents in a few swallows, and then shoved a hand into his hair, dragging slow fingers through it.

This "let's not talk about it" attitude wasn't Kat. She always told him the truth, no matter how painful, and he did the same for her. And the only thing that had changed was the sex. Which meant it was already messing things up. She was awkward and self-conscious, holding things back, keeping her thoughts to herself. He didn't like this new Kat, not one bit.

With a scowl he shifted in the chair and tried to get comfy. Pretty soon, the wind outside lulled him and he managed to fall asleep.

Four

Marco was the first to wake. After glancing at the still-sleeping Kat, he quickly checked his phone—no signal—placed it back on the table and then cast an eye at the softly glowing lights, before to Kat, now yawning on the couch. She was rubbing her cheek where the cushion had imprinted, looking so adorably sleepy that for one crazy second, impossible thoughts of permanently waking up next to her rushed through his brain and his breath caught.

"What time is it?" she asked, voice hoarse with sleep.

"Seven a.m.," he replied, glancing away. Desperate for something to do, he grabbed his phone again, determined not to focus on the way her long legs swung from the couch to the floor, her normally straight hair all mussed up and her half-lidded eyes still languorous. And of course, his mind latched on to the one thing he'd been trying to avoid. *That* moment. That hot, amazing moment on the couch when she'd crumbled beneath him.

"Phones are still out," he said, then turned the radio up.

Pretty soon they were up-to-date with the full aftermath of Cyclone Rory.

"The ports are closed, then," Kat concluded, combing her fingers through her hair.

"And there's no planes going in or out, apart from emergency ones." Marco rose, stretched and cracked his back, working his knee firmly back and forth.

"You okay?"

"Mmm."

She studied him for a moment. "Does it still ache?"

"Only when I sit for too long."

"Must be weird having pins in your knee."

He smiled thinly. "You get used to it. Could have been worse."

She nodded, knowing exactly what he meant. The on-field injury had ended one stellar career but he was lucky—it could've left him unable to walk. The bitterness still burned sometimes but it was something he refused to dwell on, not when all the other amazing opportunities had opened up for him a few months later.

"There'll be debris in the water, so they'll have to clear that up first," he continued.

"So we're stuck here until further notice."

"Until they give water traffic the all clear in a few days." At her unexpected smile, he tilted his head. "What?"

"I could name at least a dozen women who'd give their left leg to be holed up on a private island with you."

He sighed. "Why do you do that, Kat?"

"Do what?" She looked confused.

"Always bring up the women."

"I…"

She looked so genuinely flustered that his irritation quickly dissolved, leaving only an odd frustration. He sighed. "Look, forget it. We should go and see if there's any damage to the boat."

"I was only teasing."

"I know." When he held out his hand, her brief hesitation before she firmly grasped it and stood was telling.

It only increased that vague sense of wrongness.

He walked down the hall, a half-formed scowl on his face until he swung open the front door and their attention was immediately commanded by the outside world.

The warm air was rife with the smell of rain and dirt. The blue sky was cloudless, the sun already streaming through the trees to heat everything up. The palm trees still stood, but many were leafless; downed branches and debris were strewn over every inch of wet ground. As they stood there, taking in the damage, the familiar screech of rainbow lorikeets as they returned to their nests echoed.

Marco waited until they were in the buggy, making their way carefully down to the dock, before he said softly, "You know it'll be different with your own child, right?"

Her gaze snapped to him but he kept his focus ahead, avoiding the fallen branches and clumped mountains of dirt the rain had swept across the road.

"Will it?"

"Sure it will. *Je vous le*—"

"So help me, Marco, if you say that stupid catch-phrase I will seriously do you damage."

He snapped his mouth shut but couldn't completely keep the amusement from his voice. "Still don't like it, huh?"

"*Je vous le garantis.* I can guarantee it? It's lame. No one can guarantee something."

"The press seems to think so. Everyone awaits my game predictions with bated breath."

"Full of yourself much?" She snorted. "And you *have* called it wrong before."

"Only you would remember that. Three times in two years," he reminded her, grinning as he saw her mouth quirk. "Uh—I saw that smile."

"Was not a smile."

"Sure it was." He glanced at her. "I hate seeing you so serious and angry, *chérie.*"

She crossed her arms and stared right ahead, her mouth twitching. "Keep your eye on the road. There's debris all over the place."

They finally reached the windswept dock, the trees familiarly bare, the water full of flotsam. But thankfully, his boat was still moored securely, bobbing in the water, jammed up against the jetty.

He cast an eye over the lines from bow to stern, then made his way on board to inspect further. Ten minutes later, satisfied there was no damage, they returned to the house.

It was only after they returned to the house, opened all the shutters and then went back outside to inspect the filthy pool that Kat's stomach began to rumble so violently the ache made her wince.

"I need food," she said as they walked in the patio door.

"Sure." Marco moved to the kitchen. "What do you feel like?"

"I can do it."

He huffed a sigh. "Seriously? What, you've had lessons since I was last home?"

"Don't be facetious," she sniffed.

"You haven't. Which means *I'll* cook. You—" he glanced over toward the bench "—do your usual and make the coffee."

"Fine." She opened the cupboard and grabbed the gourmet coffee beans, then the grinder. It felt so surreal, going through the motions of this familiar task when all around them everything had lost grip on reality. A cyclone had raged over the coast, devastating lives. A once-strong friendship had cracked from one impulsive night. And a baby would change their lives forever.

Stop. She stared at the grinder as it tossed the beans. She couldn't make that decision yet, not when the test results were still to come.

With that tiny mantra echoing in her head, they made breakfast then ate at the table, watching the TV reports outlining the damage, filling them in on every single detail, flashing up familiar scenes of devastation, until Kat's head buzzed with overload. She glanced at Marco and then away, focusing on her plate until the silence began to cloy and she was desperate to break it.

When it got unbearable, she finally said, "So, I hear you're up for a Hall of Fame award at the FFA dinner next month."

He nodded. "Yep."

"You taking anyone?" she asked casually.

When his gaze met hers, she winced. That totally

sounded as if she was fishing, when it was definitely not the case.

"You, if you want."

"Sure." Her response was automatic. The Football Federation of Australia's annual awards dinner, a three-course dinner in a five-star Sydney hotel, was always a good night. Ironically, in a nation where sport ruled supreme, soccer barely rated a mention on the national networks, and that included the biggest soccer awards event of the year. Which suited her low-key life down to the ground.

June. Three weeks away. *Three weeks plus ten weeks means...* She scowled. *No. Don't think about that.* "So you're staying in Australia until then?"

He nodded. "I have the coaching clinics to set up, plus a new shoot for Skins. And a guest appearance on *The Big Game* when the new season starts in October."

She smiled. "Still in demand. I knew that knee injury wouldn't slow you down."

His mouth curved. "Always right, aren't you?"

"Always."

As they finished their food, Kat asked, "So what else is news?" Marco took such a long time to answer that she glanced up from her empty plate with a frown.

"Ruby's on the cover of next month's *Playboy*," he finally said.

Oh. She waited for him to share, and eventually, with a clatter of fork on plate and a deep sigh, he did. "She's my ex-wife. I shouldn't care what she does."

Kat nodded. "True."

"We've been apart for four years, divorced for two."

"Yes."

He sighed, linking his fingers together on the table.

"Call me old-fashioned, but I draw the line at having my ex-wife's hoo-ha on display for every guy who's got ten bucks to spare. Those things are private."

She looked him straight in the eye. "I agree."

He picked up the fork and continued to toy with the remains of his food in silence for a few more moments. "She didn't even ask me. I don't care about the whole media thing. I just would've liked to be forewarned."

She nodded again, knowing that the situation cut deeper than he let on. It wasn't about the damage to his reputation, although the media attention had already started to swell following the sneak peek of Ruby's cover two days ago. It was more personal than that. It went to the core of who Marco was—a deeply honorable man who respected women, who valued manners and was known in the French *futball* league as a true gentleman, despite his multitude of girlfriends and on-field arrogance.

"You know, we should get married."

She stilled, the fork halfway to her mouth. "I'm sorry. Did you just say...we should get *married*?"

He nodded, his expression deadly serious as he leaned in. "Totally."

She gaped for one second. "Why?"

He stared at her, as if waiting for her to say something more. But when she just continued to gape at him in shocked silence, he shrugged and said, "Why not?"

Because you should be madly in love with me when you propose. Kat swallowed the words as her brow dipped. "Because we don't have to?"

"So you're *not* worried about your pregnancy hitting the papers?" He tipped his head.

"Of course I am. I'm worried about everything hitting the papers. But I can't live my life in a bubble be-cause of it." She eyed him. "Anyway, what does that have to do with marriage?"

"Because we can lessen the damage. If we—"

She held up a hand. "I'm sorry, what?"

He sighed. "Look, just hear me out. For over twenty years you've not shown one symptom, so let's assume the results are negative until otherwise proven, okay? Like it or not, marriage is still a respectable option. You'll be pregnant with my child. Once the cyclone news dies down, the press will be on the lookout for the next big story, and they're going to love this. The atten-tion they give it will be off the charts. They'll hound you, your family, and when they find out I'm the father, they'll come after me." He held up a hand, cutting her off. "The papers are going to rehash every romantic in-volvement, including our marriages and divorces. And you can bet they'll find a way to bring my father into it. Someone at my network is going to listen to all that crap, and there'll probably be repercussions because I do have a code-of-conduct clause in my contract. Grace will probably demand an exclusive. The attention will drag on and on. Even better, they'll bring the romantic 'holed up during a cyclone' angle into it."

"Marco—"

"Now think about the alternative. We get married in a private ceremony then put out a press statement. The deed is done. Everything's announced how we want it, when we want it. The media have their story for a week, two, max. We'd have to tell Grace, of course, but there'll be no backlash for me at the network, no comparisons to the past. And everyone returns to their normal lives."

She stared at him for a moment and then slowly placed her fork on the plate. "It's not that simple."

"Well, obviously not." He followed with a frown. "It won't stop the attention, but it will lessen the time we'll spend on the front page. Then they'll go back to real news."

She shook her head slowly. "You would seriously marry me?"

He shrugged. "Why not?"

She said nothing, just stared at him for the longest time. She'd be Marco's wife. Mrs. Corelli. For one second her heart swooped, an alarming response that sent her into a panic before she swallowed and it all crashed back down to reality. He wanted to marry her, but for all the wrong reasons. Duty. Respectability. To avoid publicity. Not because of love.

Wait, what?

This was Marco here. He didn't think of her in that way. Oh, she knew he loved her, but he wasn't *in* love with her, which was a huge difference.

Anyway, she didn't want him in love with her. Not at all.

"You know it makes sense," he said, chewing on the last piece of toast.

There were those annoying words again. *Sensible. Smart. Logical.* Everything she'd wished for after Ezio's betrayal. Everything Marco was offering.

She drew in a slow breath. "I don't want to get married."

"What, ever again?" His brow went up. "Or just to me?"

"I've done it twice already."

"I know, *chérie*. I was there to pick up the pieces, remember?"

Her heart squeezed. Yeah, he was. He was always there. Through the divorces, the horrific tabloid attention. Through the aftermath of her mother's illness. He was her rock, more dependable than any of her girlfriends or family. He'd dropped everything to listen to her rant, then cry, then get solidly drunk and make a complete fool of herself at some swanky French nightclub. Then he'd dragged her backpacking around Europe in blissful anonymity.

And now he was offering again, stepping up and taking on the responsibility for their one lapse in judgment.

"I can't marry you, Marco," she said now. "That would be selfish."

"Why? I suggested it. And it's not as if we have anyone else lined up."

"Oh, that makes me feel so special."

He laughed, much to her chagrin. "You are. You're my closest friend."

"What about Grace?"

He sighed. "What about her? We're over, I told you. It's all in her head."

She crossed her arms and leaned back in the chair, trying to get a grip on her jumbled thoughts. "Marco, this isn't the solution. I don't want to force you into something you'll come to resent. No, let me finish," she added when he opened his mouth. "You love your freedom. You love being able to pick up and go away on assignment. I totally get that. But I need someone constant, to really *be here*. Fly-by parenting doesn't work. I know that firsthand. A child can't just be an appointment in your schedule, someone you see whenever you have a spare few weeks."

He stared at her for the longest time, until he ran a hand through his hair in frustration, his eyes narrowing. "That's ridiculous."

"Which part?"

"Oh, just about all of it." He braced his hands wide apart on the table and pinned her with his dark gaze. "Don't tell me what I feel, Kat. Sure, I love my job, but it's just a job."

"Are you kidding me? Soccer is your life. It's a part of who you are. You would die if you couldn't do it."

"You say that like I'd be giving it up. Which I'm not."

She sighed. "And we're back to where we started. Being Marco Corelli takes you all over the world. You'll be away from your child for months on end." *Away from me.* She prudently swallowed those words.

"So what's stopping you from coming with me?"

She blinked. "I have a job, in case you've forgotten." Boy, he just didn't let up, did he? Her head whirled with all the scenarios, emotions running riot until she had to take a mental step back. It was all just speculation, pipe dreams. She couldn't make a decision based on that, not when she might not even have a future.

The black moment engulfed her, stealing her breath so suddenly she shoved to her feet.

It was too, too much.

"I can't think. I need some air." Without waiting for his response, she turned and walked down the hall to her room.

Thoughts still churning, she pulled open a drawer and rummaged through the clothes she'd left from her last visit. She took a denim skirt and white linen shirt from the chest of drawers, slathered on sunscreen and then swiftly changed. When she emerged fifteen minutes later, Marco was nowhere to be seen.

After digging out sunglasses from her handbag and picking up yesterday's newspaper, she stalked over to the patio doors and slid them open, thankful Marco was not around.

That was good, wasn't it? It meant a respite from the questions she had no answers to. A break from thinking for once. And a reprieve from those annoying emotional responses that kept hijacking her thoughts whenever he smiled, shoved back his hair or touched her...or...

Simply breathed, it seemed.

With a deep sigh, she stepped outside. The tiles that ringed the eternity lap pool warmed her feet and the morning air teased over her bare arms, making her hairs stand on end.

Blinding sun speared across the deep blue ocean, the sky unmarred by clouds. She shoved on her sunglasses and assessed the now-familiar storm debris scattered over the deck and tiles, the leaves and filth floating in the pool, and then padded over to the small storage room, removed a broom and pool skimmer and set to work.

It was good to have something to do, and she set to her cleaning task with singular concentration. The sun shone brightly down, making her sweat through her shirt as she first swept the deck and surrounding tiles, then took up the skimmer and went to the pool. By the end of the repetitive skim-and-tip, her shoulders pleasantly ached and her brow was damp. Finally, she walked over to a lounge chair and settled back with the paper.

Five minutes, that was all it took, and her mind

began to drift back to what she'd effectively avoided the past hour.

With a sigh she closed the newspaper, folded it and stuck it under her leg.

"Test results aside, do you want a baby?" she asked herself aloud now, as if by voicing the question, she was giving it the proper gravitas.

"I don't know. Maybe." Pause. "Kat," she added, her voice dipping lower as if she was conducting a self-interview, "are you thinking about what others think again, and not what *you* think?"

Yeah, she was. Her father would be livid when he found out she was pregnant. The press would have a field day with this seemingly unsurprising return to form. Grace would… Well, she wasn't exactly sure what her boss would do.

On the flip side, Connor and Luke would offer support and be happy if she was, and honestly, their opinion meant more to her than all the others put together.

"Just forget about the test results for a second and think. Would having a child make you happy?"

With a sigh she recalled that odd thought from a few weeks back, the one where she'd allowed her mind free rein and had imagined a home and husband and a family.

Oh, Lord. Her breath hitched as her chest tightened, sending her emotions haywire. Maybe it was the aftermath from the storm. Maybe it was because she'd suppressed so many urges for so long. Or maybe it was because deep down inside, she didn't want to be that woman whom everyone pitied, who projected a fierce "I don't care" attitude, but inside died every time someone made a joke about her staunch opposition to having kids.

She'd thrown herself into researching motor neuron when her mother was first diagnosed with the debilitating disease that attacked the muscles but left the mind clear. The statistics, the chances of survival, the death rate… It broke her heart piece by tiny piece with every detail she'd uncovered. So after a few weeks of agony, she'd bundled up the research papers, untagged all the bookmarks and cleared her computer history, then solemnly made the choice not to get tested.

She'd come to terms with that decision, even made her peace with it. Outwardly, she'd projected that capable-career-woman persona, had brushed off any discussions about family and babies. Of course, her mother's illness wasn't a huge secret, but she'd refused to let that be a reason for people's pity. To the outside world, she'd made a conscious decision to remain childless. If everyone wanted to pour scorn on her because of that, that was their choice. Her skin was tough—she could handle it.

But now…

A baby. A family.

"Emotional stuff is scary," she said to herself now and then paused.

She sat back on the lounge, blinking out over the ocean view. There. She'd said it. It was *scary.* Opening herself up meant she'd be vulnerable. She'd done it so many times with relationships, and it was getting harder and harder to get over it when they inevitably ended. Most often badly, too.

She'd opened up once before, when she'd revealed to Ben why she didn't want kids, and he'd asked her for a divorce via text the next day.

Hang on. This is Marco we're talking about. Marco would never hurt her. He got her as no other guy did. He understood her offbeat pop-culture references, and he sang along to the music she played in her car. He let her choose the movie more often than not, and he discussed, argued and laughed with her.

He was her perfect partner.

She sat up abruptly, alarm tightening her muscles. No. Definitely not. She would *not* go there, not with him. He was her friend, not a future ex. She was supposed to be thinking about this baby, not romanticizing a one-way attraction.

"Right," she huffed, shoving her hair off her sweaty neck. "The baby. Think about the baby."

She paused. Okay, since when had she started thinking about it as an actual baby?

With a soft groan she tipped her head back. "You're going to keep it, then?"

She let that question hang in the midmorning air, the wind picking up around her, rustling the trees. The parrots squawked, the only sound punctuating the silence, and she placed a hand over her stomach and closed her eyes, cautiously giving her imagination free rein.

A baby. A miniature of her and Marco—a gorgeous child with wild curls, a beautiful mouth and high cheekbones. Marco's dreamy brown eyes…or maybe hers— sharp blue to contrast with masses of black hair. A fierce, adventurous child with charm and attitude. A combination of both, but also entirely unique, not a black-and-white copy but one that had been enhanced with color and shape and form.

She felt the catch in her throat and was helpless to stop it, until it came out as a gasping sob.

She wanted this baby. She *actually* wanted it.

Wow.

After all those years of not caring, not wanting. She wanted. It was like an epiphany, a shiny new revelation that actually made perfect sense the more she thought about it.

Marco was right: things would be different with her child. Yes, the prospect of becoming a mother was scary, different and way out of her comfort zone.

She'd never allowed herself the luxury of thinking about a family. She was Katerina Jackson. She'd handled paparazzi, the crème de la crème of society, weird celebrities and total-jerk boyfriends. She'd come through two divorces a stronger person. She was fortunate enough to have money, friends and support. And when the blood tests from the geneticist came back negative, the only obstacle remaining would be gone.

"A mother," she said softly, skimming a hand over her still-flat belly. "Me. That's…incredible."

She had to tell Marco.

Five

Kat swiveled her feet to the tiles and stood, then padded across the courtyard and back into the house.

"Marco?"

Loud in the silence, her voice echoed off the walls. She tilted her head and paused, her brow furrowing in concentration as she listened.

Was that…music? Violin, to be exact.

Her frown deepened. Marco liked a collection of hard rock, Europop and Top 40, but he'd never professed a great love of classical. She slowly followed the thread down the corridor to the closed doors that led to the indoor pool and paused, her hand resting lightly on the sliding door's handle.

He was obviously in a private moment. The verticals were drawn, door closed, music cranked up.

And yet this had to be done.

Before she could talk herself out of it, she clicked the handle and walked in.

Just like all the times before, this room stole her breath away. The low whitewashed arches, the concrete floor with Grecian tiles leading to a kidney-shaped heated pool, the fully stocked wet bar in the middle. And to the right, an intimate entertaining alcove that always made her think dirty thoughts.

Dirty thoughts that suddenly morphed into reality when she spotted Marco lying shirtless, listening to music.

Oh, God. She sucked in a silent breath, frozen in her tracks. He was facing her, his eyes shut tight, expression creased in concentrated passion and his hand moving through the air as he focused on the piece—a beautiful, haunting piece that made her heart swell and thump, a soft groan sticking in her throat as it echoed off the walls.

She ran her gaze hungrily over his figure, from those jet-black curls, noble nose and defined jaw, to shoulders of corded muscle, broad chest, ridged abdomen and lean waist. By the time she'd reached his firm thighs, encased in pants, she'd become more than a little hot. Who would've guessed that watching him as he listened to the music—his expression moving in rhythm, his hand conducting as the notes went through the dips and troughs—would be so arousing?

But damn, it was. It was as if her insides had suddenly been set on slow burn, and coupled with the hot music as an erotic sound track, everything began to slowly melt, making her steadily damp the longer she stood there and stared.

And stare she did. It was as though the music possessed him, commanded him. Touched him. And she couldn't look away from his expression as it moved and morphed, his hand swaying in time.

She'd never been turned on so much in her life.

Then the song abruptly finished, his eyes springing open on the very last note, and she was caught standing there gawping like some weird, obsessive stalker.

He noticed her almost immediately, so she couldn't even preserve their dignity by retreating. His dark eyes fixed on her, his expression blank as he stared for long moments, a light sheen of sweat glistening under the soft overhead lights. Slowly, he wiped his brow, shoving his hair off his forehead, and Kat's mouth went dry.

Marco was her best friend. He infuriated her. He made her laugh, made her yell. He was her rock, her shoulder to cry on. And she was his plus one whenever he needed her, his sometimes clothing consultant, drinking buddy, confidante. Of course she loved him, just as she loved Connor and Luke.

But now, as he sat there and stared right back at her, residual emotion slowly bleeding from his expression, all she could think about was how much she wanted him.

He was glorious. A perfect example of passion and beauty, all wrapped up in dark Botticelli curls and a classic European profile that had women swooning even before he opened his mouth and that dreamy French accent came out.

She twisted her fingers in the ties of her shirt and said faintly, "Since when have you been interested in classical music?"

He slowly stood. "Since last year."

"And you didn't tell me?"

He shrugged.

Odd. "What was that piece called?" She forged on with a small frown.

"*Idylle sur la Paix* by Jean-Baptiste Lully." He absently plucked at the hem of his trouser leg.

"Never heard of him."

"Seventeenth-century French dancer and musician. He invented baroque music."

"Oh." She smiled. "No one important, then."

His mouth quirked. "He was King Louis XIV's court composer—a musical genius who also knew how to get what he wanted. Best friends with playwright Molière. A fascinating character, but unfortunately there's not a lot about him, unlike Mozart or Beethoven."

"That's a shame."

"I've got a couple of books and a French movie, but not much else." He slowly reached for the stereo remote and clicked it off. "You should see the movie—you'd like it." He smiled. "Especially the costumes. Historically inaccurate but still flamboyant."

"You'd have to translate for me."

"I could do that." He dragged a hand across his chin then put both hands on his hips, and Kat couldn't help but linger on all that casually exposed skin—the taut shoulders, the defined ridges of his abdomen, that tempting Adonis belt disappearing beneath his waistband.

Her heart began to canter and her mouth was dry when she finally met his gaze. His expression was unreadable, but his eyes darkened in an oh-so-familiar way as he leisurely took in her warm face and neck, then farther down to her torso partially exposed by her shirt. He finally finished his perusal at her legs before returning to her face, and her fingers involuntarily clenched hard into fists.

"Kat..."

Her name tripped so deliciously off his tongue in that beautiful accent, and she was gone. He must have realized it, too, because all he had to do was hold out a hand and crook his finger in a "come here" gesture and she leaped to do his bidding.

She walked, slowly and purposefully, around the edge of the pool, her bare feet on the cool tiles a welcome relief compared with the warmth curling in her belly.

When she finally stood before him, her lungs emptied on a shaky breath. *Lush:* that was the perfect word to describe Marco Corelli. Lush and romantic, especially with those dark curls and perfect lips.

He'd be a hit, of that she was sure.

She held her breath as he slowly reached out and curled a lock of her hair around his finger, tugging gently on it for a moment before pushing it behind her ear.

Then he leaned in, inch by agonizing inch, until his mouth was a whisper away from hers and she could feel his warm breath feather across her skin.

"Kat," he murmured, his dark hooded eyes dropping to her mouth, then back up to her eyes.

She swayed, every single cell in her body tingling from anticipation, breath rattling low in her throat. "Yes?"

"Kiss me."

With a soft groan she jerked forward, demolishing the divide between them and bringing her lips to his.

His mouth was warm and tasted faintly of peppermint. As she pressed her lips urgently against his, she heard a moan low in his throat a second before his hands were on her shoulders, dragging her to his chest.

Yes. She felt the excited flush sweep her from head to toe and, with another groan, put her arms around his neck and deepened the kiss.

Breath mingling. Hearts racing. Skin heating. It all happened in an instant, as if her body had been waiting for this exact moment to spark to life. When his tongue expertly parted her mouth, diving inside to tangle with hers, she gasped, legs wobbling, and immediately his arms tightened, taking all of her weight as her insides melted. They stood like that for ages, tasting each other, the room echoing with soft moans and heavy breathing. And finally, after she'd been thoroughly and skillfully aroused just short of the point of frustration, he began backing her up to the daybed.

She went willingly, clinging to him while his mouth continued to make her breathless. He took her bottom lip between his and gently sucked, his hands sliding down her lower back to firmly cup her bottom then press her urgently into him.

She gasped, feeling the hardness of his arousal against her clothes. The sudden urgent desire to be naked, to have him cover her, have him inside her, flamed.

"Marco," she groaned as her legs hit the edge of the bed.

"Hmm?" His lips were trailing over her jaw, then down her neck, and when they hit her most sensitive spot where her neck met her shoulder, she sucked in a gasp.

"Take your pants off."

She felt his mouth curve on her neck just before his hands went to his waistband, quickly unsnapping his pants and dragging them down, and she barely had time for the reality to sink in—*Marco is getting naked!*—before he went for her clothes.

Soon she was shirtless, and he was pressed up against her, his mouth returning to hers for a deep, breathless kiss before he slowly made his way down her neck.

She swallowed thickly, the heat from his lips trailing small shudders across her skin. Dimly she was aware of her bra being removed, and then he was pushing her gently down onto the bed, his hand cupping one breast. Her back curved, arching into his touch, and with a soft murmur he obliged, his thumb sweeping over one peaking nipple before he took it in his mouth and sucked.

She shuddered, which was unbelievable considering the amount of control she normally had over every single waking moment of the day. But with Marco it was different. He had suddenly become chaos in her ordered world, and she was experiencing all sorts of things for the first time. As his mouth and tongue worked magic on her skin, coaxing her nipple into an achingly hard peak, she shoved any doubts she had into the back of her mind and just let the moment take her.

Her hands went to his boxers, hooking her thumbs in the waistband then slowly taking them off. And when she reached for him, his soft exclamation in her ear only fueled her desire.

Then he leaned back and her eyes flew open to stare into his dark depths.

"Kat…" he groaned, expression twisting. "Do you want to…? Should I…?"

Her breath came out slowly, heavily, as she cupped

his face with one hand, emotion and desire and need roiling in her stomach in one heated mass.

"Yes." She placed a soft kiss on his mouth. "I need you." Her teeth gently captured his bottom lip. "Deep." She sucked on his lip, her breath ragged, matching his. "Slow." Darting her tongue out, she licked the curve of his mouth. "Please."

His eyes closed on a thick gasp, and she watched his throat work, swallowing slowly. Then his knee was nudging her thighs apart. When his hand went between her legs, her body jerked.

His long, skillful fingers teased and tempted, his thumb coaxing the swelling nub of her arousal over and over as she trembled with every stroke, rocking her hips into his hand, grinding firmly as she whimpered beneath his mouth. With a low chuckle he continued, sliding first one finger inside, then another, working her with a steady, sensual glide that swiftly reduced her to a quivering mass of need.

"Marco!" She was beyond caring how desperate she sounded, how much she needed him, how damp he made her. Because right now, all that existed was his mouth, his hand…and suddenly, his throbbing manhood as he swiftly positioned himself and pushed inside with one hard thrust.

Oh…! Everything shorted out, until all that was left was thick heat and a hard pounding heartbeat echoing inside every single nerve. And when he slowly shifted his hips and inched deeper, she gasped, eyes flying open to meet his.

His face, that beautiful face, was so close to hers she could smell the arousal rolling off him. Her entire body pulsed from it, hot and breathless. How could she

withstand these sensations, this glorious heat, the tightness, the pure friction of taking him deep inside her?
Then he moved again and she knew she'd do more than
withstand it. She'd revel in it, enjoy the pure moment
of claiming him in the most primitive way possible.

She groaned, rocking back to meet his thrusts, the
friction of him steadily flaming her arousal. Her thick-
ened heartbeat throbbed wildly in her head, and she
pushed back into him, hard, squeezing her eyes shut,
groaning. "Marco…"

"Hmm?"

Instead of answering, she grabbed his hand, sliding
it to where they were intimately joined. "There. Touch
me there."

He did as she asked, moving his fingers over the
hot, sensitive nub of her arousal. "Oh, yes…" She bit
down on her lip, her hand still on his, losing herself in
the sensation of his fingers, his mouth on her nipple
and him hard inside her as he slowly and firmly moved.

They remained that way for excruciating minutes,
rocking together, his finger flicking her intimately over
and over, until she was sure she'd explode from it all.
And then he surprised her by suddenly flipping her onto
her stomach, looping a hand under her hips and pulling
her up onto all fours. Before her brain could register the
interruption, his hand swept over her butt. He nudged
her legs apart and entered her from behind.

Her breath came out in a harsh gasp, and she had to
brace her hands wide on the mattress to accommodate
all of him. He paused, a palm gently sweeping over the
curve of one butt cheek.

"Kat? Are you okay?"

Was she okay? Hell, no. She was about to die from

every single piece of her exploding in joy. Instead, she managed to get out, "Yes…yes."

"You sure?" His hand stroked her back, her hip, before slowly easing around her waist to cup one breast.

"I won't be if you don't keep going."

His chuckle—partly amused, partly dirty—nearly did her in. Instead she pushed back into him and felt no small satisfaction in hearing his harsh intake before he gripped her hips and began to rock.

She gasped as sensation took over; she felt his mouth as he leaned over and bit gently on her shoulder, his hands firmly cupping her breasts, and the hot, sweet sensation of him deep inside, filling her completely, creating such an arousing, intimate friction that a whimper welled deep in her throat.

Then it hit and she went down to her elbows, unable to hold back as the shuddering release swept her entire body, and she heaved in great gulping breaths, welcoming his weight as everything pulsed in pleasure.

"Marco…" For the third time, his name ripped from her mouth, like a mantra, and she felt the stinging sensation of his teeth grazing her neck, then her name echoed and the room filled with their harsh cries of release.

Dimly, she was aware that she'd collapsed on the bed, and Marco's body was flush on hers, damp and heavy in the aftermath of passion.

"That was… You are…" She groaned into the mattress, chest heaving.

His hand went to her face, gently turning her to him, his mouth seeking hers. "Kiss me."

She did, sweetly and softly, and a groan escaped his lips when he finally broke away, lifting his body off hers. "Sorry. I'm way too heavy to be lying on you, especially when…"

He petered off, letting her fill in the blank, which she did way too quickly.

It was a definite mood killer.

She sighed, watching him move around the shadowed room, picking up his boxers and pulling them on. With a flush she glanced away from his perfect form—long, corded thighs; strong, muscular back; and perfectly shaped behind.

"Marco, we need to talk."

He finally turned to her, hands on hips, and she couldn't help steal a brief glance at his chest before quickly forcing her gaze to his eyes.

She didn't know what she expected—amusement over her perusal, a sarcastic eye roll over the clichéd relationship line they both hated. Even residual lust wouldn't have been unusual. But there was none of that, only a carefully blank countenance that accompanied the vague sense of anticipation in the air.

"I think we should."

Right. So far, so good. She gathered the sheet around her, covering her breasts, before continuing. "Okay, so I don't want to make any major decisions without the test results, but I do know one thing. If the tests turn out to be negative, I want to keep the baby."

The silence fell like a blanket, and yet he still said nothing, just waited for her to elaborate. The simple fact that he knew there *was* more was as unnerving as it was disturbing.

"And here's the thing, Marco," she continued. "I don't want this child to have a part-time parent. You're either totally in this or not at all."

He frowned. "What makes you think I'm not in this?"

She sighed. "I don't want you making major decisions based on what *I* want. You want to go back to France, you go."

The frustrated growl was low in his throat. "You can't throw out something like that and then tell me *not* to think about what you want. That's not the way I operate."

"I know. But you have to. I'm giving you permission to walk away from all the craziness now."

"You're not making any kind of sense." He raked her with such a look that she felt her cheeks flush. "First you say I should be in this totally or not at all. Then you say I should do what I like." His hands went to his hips, his expression darkening. "Let me ask you this—knowing me so well, do you actually think I'd walk away?"

"That's not what I'm saying."

"Oh, that's exactly what you're saying." His expression remained tight, almost too tight. "That's pretty low, Kat. Thanks. Thanks a lot."

She blinked. Had she hurt him? His face said no, yet the brief flash in his eyes said the opposite. "I just…" She swallowed when she saw his scowling countenance. "I don't want you to feel trapped."

"How long have we known each other?"

She paused, calculated. "Nineteen years."

"Right. And in all that time, have you known me to do something I didn't want to do?"

She hesitated. "No."

"There you go." He yanked on his pants, slid up the zipper.

"But—"

"Dear Lord, Kat, can you stop? Just…stop." He finished dressing, then gave her a frustrated look. "If all you're going to do is lump me in with past boyfriends, then I'm going for a shower."

She opened her mouth for a second and then closed it. "Great. Fine. Go."

He narrowed his eyes. "So we're done here? You've said everything you need to?"

"Looks like it." She scooted to the edge of the bed with as much dignity as possible, anger welling up inside. But when he stalked out in long, ground-eating strides, she collapsed back on the mattress. Could it be more uncomfortable? From best friends to arguing lovers in the space of a day.

Must be some kind of record for her.

This wasn't what she wanted. Not at all. But how in the hell could she fix it?

Good Lord, Kat was so stubborn.

Marco was in the kitchen, gathering up food and utensils for lunch with more noise than necessary, his thoughts dark, before moving onto the patio, to the huge four-burner barbecue.

She was so determined to make her own decisions, to not even consider a different opinion unless she'd thought of it first.

Sure, his long absences from home were sometimes inconvenient, and there were times when he felt he was playing catch-up with people's lives. But after his knee injury had forced him into early retirement and the network had offered him this prime job, he'd jumped at the opportunity. And from that choice, a whole new bunch of opportunities had opened up—his Skins contract, the football clinics. He couldn't afford to regret any of it, not when things were as pretty close to perfect as he could get.

But right now, at this moment? A flame of frustration had flickered to life, refusing to be quenched.

Damn, he missed everyone, missed being able to drop everything and catch up with a meal and a beer. But with Luke and Connor in Brisbane and he and Kat up here in Cairns, plus their work commitments, it was a logistical nightmare trying to sync their schedules.

With an irritated flick he threw the steaks onto the hot plate, his bad mood momentarily rewarded by the satisfying hiss.

For example, if they were all together right now, they'd have this issue picked apart and solved within an hour. Instead of what had really happened—his making a lame marriage proposal, her getting all offended for some reason and now this weird standoff.

After a few minutes of grilling the hell out of the steaks, a movement through the glass caught his eye. He turned to see Kat standing in the middle of the living room, her attention commanded by the TV.

The sight hit him low and hard. She was barefoot and wide-eyed, looking sexily rumpled in nothing but short-shorts and an old gray T-shirt that skimmed her thighs. Magnificent thighs.

His head flashed back to what they'd done in the pool room. Then, further, to the larger issues they were both determined to avoid until hard evidence left them no choice.

He scowled. He'd never craved—yet dreaded—the outcome of a test so much in his life. The knowledge would change their lives forever, for the better or the absolute worst, and it wasn't until this moment that he understood why Kat had deliberately chosen the path of not knowing. It took a strong person to fight, but it also took someone equally strong to choose the other path, to live their lives with impunity when somewhere, in the back of their minds, they would always be wondering, thinking, considering.

Kat was way stronger than he even thought possible.

Humbled and angry, he turned his attention back to the grill and waited for her to approach him.

He hadn't long to wait—a few minutes was all it took.

"Can I do anything?" she asked, standing in the open door.

He glanced up briefly then back to the grill. "We need drinks."

"Sure."

He watched her pad to the kitchen, his eyes skimming over her long legs. He took in the way her back remained firm and straight, and he swallowed the lump in his throat.

Quickly he served up the steaks then went inside.

When she took the plate he offered, a whiff of scent hit him, tightening his gut. "What are you wearing?"

She glanced down and plucked at the T-shirt. "This? It's a sleeping shirt."

"No. Your perfume."

"Oh." She looked disconcerted for a second then said faintly, "Lemongrass and cloves. I keep it in my underwear...drawer..."

Her words trailed off at the exact same moment he grinned. He could practically read her thoughts—*Great,*

Kat, just talk about your knickers, why don't you?—and his mouth curved wider.

"Is that enough?" Marco said.

"Hmm?"

He nodded at her steak. "Do you have enough?"

She swallowed. "Yes, thanks."

He watched her take a seat at the table, her gaze darting up to his before she steadfastly focused on the food, and the brief moment of amusement was gone.

What the hell was wrong with…?

Riiiiight. He sat in his chair, his eyes going anywhere but to her. She was nervous. But why? He'd teased her a hundred times before, and about things a lot more personal.

Yeah, but that was Marco-the-best-friend, not Marco-the-lover. Like it or not, things had changed. It was almost as if…she was uncomfortable now.

He swallowed a curse. What the hell was he supposed to do with that?

"Kat," he said in a low voice.

"Hmm?" Her attention remained firmly on her plate.

"This is weird for me, too."

Her eyes darted to his. "What, specifically?"

"You and me."

She blinked. "Is—?" He watched her swallow. "There isn't a you and me."

Isn't there? The unspoken question just hung in the air, the seconds gathering, until he realized he was frowning, and she'd darted her gaze back to her plate.

"So we're just occasional bed partners, then."

The sarcasm was lost on her. "I don't think that's a good idea."

He stared at the top of her head in silence, and finally, reluctantly, she brought her eyes up to his and he stifled a groan. Soft skin. The indent of her waist, the curve of her butt cheek. Her damp body shaking as he took her, desire raging hard and fast. And her moans of pleasure as they both reached their climax.

His thoughts raced, nostrils flaring with remembrance, but he let the silence drag, until her eyes widened and she swept her gaze back to her plate. "You're my best friend, Marco. I don't want to ruin our friendship."

"It's not ruined. Just…" He searched for a word and finally settled on "Different."

"Different," she repeated with a small scowl.

He nodded. "Of course. We've slept together. We're having a baby. How can those things not make it different?"

"I don't *want* it different."

"You've made that perfectly clear," he snapped back and then took a breath. "But denial is stupid."

Her head jerked up. "Are you calling me stupid?"

"No! Jeez, Kat…!" His breath was sharp on the intake as he tried for calm. "I'm not calling you stupid," he said deliberately, rising from the table with his plate. "But wishing the past was different is a waste of time. You know that."

When she said nothing, just slid her gaze away and refused to meet his eyes, he swallowed a groan. It was her infuriating you're-right-but-I'm-not-going-to-admit-it look. God, that annoyed the hell out of him!

"It was fine the way it was," she said now, her gaze now on her plate.

The blow hit him like a stray free shot. She didn't want him.

No, that wasn't right—she didn't want *anyone*. She'd made that clear. He shouldn't take it personally. Yet how could he not, when they'd been together three times now and every time she'd indicated she'd rather be friends?

He knew exactly what she was doing. Things were getting emotional and she was pushing him away. She'd done it with everyone when her mother had started getting sick, and she was doing it now. Only this time, she had to deal with not only pregnancy hormones but the mental effort of waiting for those damn test results.

If this was what she really wanted, he'd let her have it...for now. He'd keep his thoughts and hands to himself, support her and stand by her as a best friend, and only that. But eventually, after they got off this island and went back to their reality, things would change. They had to. Because they'd stepped over that line and he was damned if he'd remain on the sidelines, where she was so determined to push him.

Six

The next morning Kat lay in her bed, staring at the ceiling as the sun slowly crept through the blinds.

They'd spent the evening in uncomfortable silence. Even the constant TV chatter did nothing to ease the awkwardness. She'd finally excused herself and went to bed, then lay for ages staring at the window and listening to the sounds of the night creatures rustling around outside.

Marco as her lover? Ridiculous.

Yet every time she'd lost her head, forgot who he was and just let the moment take her. It was crazy. Exciting.

Dammit, she couldn't stop those hot memories from filling her thoughts at the most inopportune moments. The way he kissed her, as if he couldn't get enough. The way he touched her, his fingers making her shiver in anticipation. And the way he took her, hard and possessive.

Yeah, and you've given him the "just friends" talk. Which he accepted without argument. She'd told him he was the father of her child, nothing more.

The question was, did she want him as more? Did she want to start something that could end in disaster? Or worse, drag him into an emotional mess when she had no clue what those damn tests would reveal?

You can't.

With a hitched breath, she rolled over in bed and hugged her pillow. This was Marco Corelli, a guy she knew better than anyone. Yet in this one thing, she had absolutely no clue.

And then there was the matter of Grace.

She groaned and gave the pillow a vicious thump. Everything was such a mess, and on top of that, she had to figure out something to tell Grace. Oh, she'd contemplated not saying a thing, but experience had taught her it was better to be honest. And anyway, she liked and respected her boss. She deserved to know.

Sorry, Grace. The guy you wanted a baby with? He's having it with me.

She winced.

Grace, I know you had plans for Marco—

Urgh. Terrible.

Grace. I need to tell you about something that happened....

She rolled her eyes. It sounded so much better in her head. Come to think of it, lots of things sounded better in her head. Truthfully, she had no idea why she was practicing—she worked much better off-the-cuff. And it was something she should really think about *after* the test results came through.

"I can't wait to get off this bloody island," she muttered.

When she walked into the living room half an hour later, the breakfast things were already laid out on the table. Marco was dressed in a white shirt and jeans and was flicking through the TV channels.

"What's the situation with the cyclone?" she asked as she sat and reached for the cereal.

"They're saying the phone towers may be up and running in a few hours," he said as he moved into the kitchen and pushed down the toaster.

"Good."

"Eager to escape, *chérie?*"

His smile lacked warmth, which only made her feel bad. "I'm eager to know the results of my tests," she said slowly as she poured the milk then grabbed her spoon.

He nodded, his attention riveted to the toaster.

"Marco…"

"Hmm?" He remained focused on his task and she bit her lip, her gaze sweeping over him before darting away.

"Nothing," she mumbled and shoved a spoonful of cereal in. "We should watch that DVD you were telling me about. After breakfast, maybe."

He glanced over at her, his expression unreadable, and then back to the toaster as it pinged. "Sure."

Just as they did yesterday, they ate in silence, their attention focused on the TV. *It's still happening,* she realized, her eyes determinedly fixed on the news updates. She hated this awkwardness, as if they were waiting for the other to address the elephant in the room.

It was excruciating.

When he got up with his plate, she couldn't help but lift her gaze to follow. He had a way of walking, a kind of fluid motion that had earned him many women admirers when he'd played for Marseille.

Actually, he still had a few.

She sighed and rose. Three times now they'd ended up in bed, and every time it still amazed her. But to voice her need, her wish to have him as a friend *and* a lover...that was too damn scary. She'd be a fool to start something, only to have it implode if the test results came back positive. Because then she'd have to deal with that on top of everything else, and she was damn sure she didn't want to put Marco through even a millionth of what she'd suffered, watching someone she loved slowly wither away.

She walked over to the sink to rinse her bowl and unthinkingly settled her soft fingers on the warm flesh of his waist to nudge him out of her way.

He jumped like a scalded cat, which in turn made her jump.

"Sorry," she said when he shot her a look. Her face was a hairbreadth away from his shoulder—within kissing distance, she realized dazedly. Yet his small shiver had her frowning as he slowly moved to her right.

"Your hair," he murmured, removing his plate from the sink. "Tickles."

"Sorry," she said again unconvincingly, leaning down to open the dishwasher. Her breath caught when her arm skimmed his chest; she knew she'd gotten to him when she heard the snag in his throat.

The heady feeling of power winded her. "You should put a jumper on."

"Huh?"

She nodded at his bare arms, now littered with goose-bumps. "If you're cold you should put a jumper on."

He sent her a closed, indecipherable look that confused as much as aroused. How on earth had she been able to look at that face, into those dark eyes, without feeling her pulse spike before? But she had. She'd hugged, laughed and touched with impunity, secure in their platonic-friend zone. But now…now all she wanted to do was touch him. Kiss him.

Get him into bed again.

With a thick swallow, she called on her thinly shredded control and turned away.

"Let's watch that movie."

From the very first minute, the very first strike of classical music booming through the speakers, she was hooked.

Of course, it was all in French and Marco had to translate. Her breath caught every time he leaned in, his deep voice soft over the lilting on-screen French. The music was rich and powerful, the costumes beautifully flamboyant, and she could feel her senses spike in response. And of course, there was Marco sitting close, his body heat and faint cologne a frustrating accompaniment to the period drama. She had to stop herself from squirming after one intimate scene, to firmly focus on the screen and not turn and kiss him as he bent in to translate a particularly hot piece of dialogue.

She swallowed, suppressed a shudder and made a move to rise. "I need a drink. Do you want a drink?"

She squeaked when his arm went around her, pulling her back down. "No. Wait until after this scene. It's awesome."

"Just let it play. I won't be a second."

He groaned and clicked Pause. "You always do that. I hate it!"

"It's only a few seconds," she said, grabbing his fingers and pulling. "Let me go."

"No. Louis is about to confront his mother. You'll miss something important."

She worked at his fingers but he held her fast, and she couldn't help but stifle a giggle. A giggle that rushed out in a gasp as he yanked and she ended up sprawled in his lap. "The drink can wait."

"But—"

"Quiet, woman. I'm trying to watch the movie and you're ruining the mood."

With an exaggerated sigh she settled her head on his thigh and watched the scene.

When Marco casually draped his arm over her waist, an involuntary shiver coursed down her back. She was suddenly very much aware that his hand was curled at her hip, his hard thigh beneath her cheek and the back of her head in his lap.

Oh, dear.

She tried to focus on the movie, but it was no good. Amid the powerful scene, full of heightened tension, coupled with Marco's soft translation, she could feel her body heat up.

Her breath hitched. She couldn't take her eyes off the screen, and she couldn't switch off her senses because Marco was everywhere—his hand resting lightly on her hip. His scent, all male and clean. And that voice, so achingly intimate that her insides just seemed to shudder every time he opened his mouth.

When she stirred, she felt his thigh beneath her cheek shift and tighten, and she had to clench her fists to stop herself from involuntarily stroking that hard muscle.

She closed her eyes, swallowing thickly as his hand suddenly left her hip to gently toy with her hair.

So soft. Marco heard her faint sigh, barely discernible against the rich baroque sound track. Yet his senses went on high alert at the sudden tension riding her back as he continued to stroke her hair, the silky chocolate strands twining around his fingers. The sudden urge to bury his face in that hair, breathe deep and never come up for air winded him.

"Marco?"

His name, warm and whispery on her lips, sent a bolt of heat to his groin.

"Yes?"

"You should stop."

He didn't pretend to fake ignorance. "I don't think I can."

She turned her head in his lap and he groaned under his breath. Her wide blue eyes stared up at him, and he couldn't help himself. He needed to kiss her. Now.

So he did.

She had ample time to protest or move away, but she did neither, just watched him get closer and closer until his lips gently brushed over hers, tentative at first, then with more urgency.

Her sigh ended on a groan and told him everything he needed to know.

They spent long moments that way, just exploring

each other's mouths with lips, tongue and breath until Marco finally pulled back with a soft curse.

"What the hell is this, Kat?"

She stared up at him, eyes wide. "I have no clue. But…can we just…not talk about it?"

"Kat—"

"Please, Marco. With everything else going on, let's just not…not analyze this."

His hand skimmed over her jaw then down her neck to finally rest across her collarbone, a frankly possessive gesture that she ignored. "We're going to have to at some point."

She sighed. "I know. Just not now, okay?"

When she tentatively leaned up, lips seeking his, he pulled back, and for one brief second he saw her tense, as if preparing herself for rejection, and it just about killed him then and there. With a groan, he cupped her head and captured her lips in a deep kiss.

They kissed for ages, the rich music and French dialogue a sensual background that only flamed his need, urging him to do more, to touch, to possess.

He abruptly pulled back. "We should…"

She swallowed. "Stop?"

"Are you asking me or telling me?"

He heard her breath rattle as he studied her, taking in the curve of her lips, the mix of emotion in her darkened eyes. Did she…? Would he…?

Impossible.

Or was it?

"You're right."

He gently eased off the couch and moved away to the kitchen, leaving her in silence. She'd surely stop him, say something, if she thought any different, right?

But as he went through the motions of getting a drink, the silence was loud and obvious.

He hadn't mistaken that look—a mix of want and trepidation. He'd seen it so often in other women.

But this was Kat. His Kat.

No, not his.

Annoyed, he lingered in the kitchen as she sat on the couch, until the unmistakable ping of his phone broke the silence.

He paused. "Did you hear that?"

"What?"

"My phone pinged."

"That means the towers are working," she said.

He frowned and then quickly strode over to his phone, flicking it on. She picked up hers and did the same, hurriedly scanning through the messages.

Disappointment curled in his belly as he read. Ridiculous. They couldn't stay here forever. They needed to get back to their lives, to reality. Which meant work, test results. Press coverage.

He groaned softly, dragging a hand over his face. God, they'd have a field day with this trapped-alone-in-a-cyclone scenario. And Grace, she'd definitely want in on that story. Then there were Kat's test results that frankly scared the crap out of him.

He glanced over and saw her staring intently at her phone and frowning. They'd all want a piece of her. She could skillfully avoid the press, but Grace… Yeah, Kat's boss was demanding and challenging. It took a special person to work for her, and he knew she bugged Kat for an exclusive at least once a week. So far she'd held out, but after the past few days he wasn't entirely sure Grace would keep taking no for an answer.

The sudden urge to escape, to take Kat somewhere where they could relax in blissful anonymity and just ignore the realities of the outside world, swept over him, and his grip tightened on the phone. Japan, maybe? The Himalayas? Alaska. Alaska was nice....

Or they could just stay here.

Her soft exclamation broke through his thoughts and he quickly busied himself with the cups.

"The geneticist called. They have my results."

He spun around, but she'd already pulled open the patio doors and stepped outside. The soft click of the door was as final as any slam.

She'd shut him out.

Damn. He busied himself with coffee, refusing to look further into it. As always, she'd tell him in her own time, and as always, he'd be there for her, whatever the result.

He paused, and damn, the panic he thought he'd managed to ignore these past few days just swept right back in, leaving him floundering in a pool of helplessness.

He couldn't lose her. Not his Kat. Not the woman he'd just realized he was totally and completely in love with.

Wait, what?

Before he had a chance to let that realization take bloom, she'd reopened the door and was standing, pale and still, in the middle of the room.

"Kat?"

"I know they're not supposed to tell you over the phone," she said slowly. "But Dr. Hardy and my mother go back a long way, and I wasn't sure when we'd return to the mainland and—" She stopped, took a deep breath and looked him in the eye. "Sorry, I'm rambling.

I just…" She dragged a hand through her hair with a sigh as he just stood there, his heart lumping in his throat, blood pounding way too loud.

"Kat, you're killing me here," he said softly. "What did he say?"

"They're doing another test, to double-check the results," she began. "But…"

"Yes?"

"Preliminary tests were…" Her eyes rounded, disbelieving. "Positive." She swallowed, her voice cracking. "They were positive."

Oh, dear God.

For one second the world stopped spinning. He realized he'd gotten out a thick "What?" but the shock quickly drowned everything else out. She was… She had…

No. Just no.

NO.

He realized he was staring, silent and disbelieving, until he saw her tears spilling, slowly coursing down her cheeks, and his heart just shattered into a million tiny pieces.

Nonononononono—

He surged forward just as she let out a gut-wrenching sob. In a few strides he'd crossed the room, and then he was crushing her against his chest.

She collapsed into him, and when he felt her begin to shake, he just held on tighter.

Impotent fury surged because he couldn't help her, couldn't stop her tears, couldn't do a damn thing but hold her, muttering totally useless sentiments while she cried and cried and broke his heart over and over.

He swallowed thick gulps of air, tightening his embrace as she trembled in his arms. She was so damn strong all the time, and it killed him to see her so broken now. After her mother's death, she'd never allowed herself to think about this possibility. She'd been determined to live her life without a death sentence tainting every moment. But now...now...

He held on tight, feeling her body shake, her tears dampening his shoulder, and he swallowed again and again, sucked it all up and bit back all his pain even as he felt his own tears spill on his cheeks. She needed him to be the strong one here. He'd be useless to her any other way.

Yet how could he when everything inside him throbbed with pain and fury and the injustice of it all?

That anger took flame, growing with each second, until thankfully he managed to force back the tears. "We'll get another test," he muttered against her hair. "And then another. They could've made a mistake—it happens all the time."

She muttered something unintelligible, and when she finally lifted her face to his, her expression so broken and torn, he couldn't help himself.

He leaned down and kissed her, hard.

She kissed him back just as fiercely, her small whimper warm in his mouth, her cheeks wet against his. When he angled her head and thrust his tongue between her lips, she groaned, welcoming him, her hands fisting in his shirt to pull him closer.

His brain shorted out as lust instantly exploded. He grabbed her arms and kept kissing her, her gasps of pleasure feathering over his lips, her hands grappling with his shirt, yanking it from his pants.

And then she was backing him up, and suddenly they

were sprawled on the couch with her on top, mouths still locked.

He couldn't think, couldn't speak. The emotion of the moment had completely hijacked any thought of common sense. With frantic hands they worked his pants open then off, then attacked her shirt, ripping it with their urgency. This was lust at its highest, the kind of clothes-ripping, skin-biting rush that left no room for soft words of love. It was just about the physical coming together of two people in desperate emotional need to connect, to prove they were still alive and were far from done yet.

He yanked up her skirt then dragged down her knickers, briefly reveling in her soft skin, in the warm, throbbing life of her, before she was bracing her hands on each side of his head. With mouths still locked in a desperate kiss, he grasped her hips, shifting her slightly, before plunging her straight down onto his aching manhood.

Her gasp rent the air and he groaned against her hot mouth, feeling the hard pulse of his arousal buried deep inside her. For a dozen breathtaking moments they remained still, intimately joined but unmoving as their eyes locked and they shared one breath.

It was…she was…incredible. Amazing.

With shaky hands, he swept his thumbs over her cheeks, sweeping away the last of her tears, before placing a slow, agonizing kiss first over one eyelid then the other.

"Kat…"

Her expression crumbled. "Please, Marco. Don't talk." Then she swooped down for a kiss, silencing him, and began to slowly, sensuously rock.

Instinctively he gripped her hips, taking charge of the rhythm, commanding her body. His heart pounded thickly, blood racing. He may have heard her whimper; he wasn't sure because his heart was beating so damn fast it felt as if the whole room echoed with it. And past that, there was the faint, sensuous sound of flesh on flesh coupled with their heavy breathing.

She rolled into him, biting her lip. "Marco…"

"Yeah?" His gaze met hers, and the raw need etched on her face blew him away.

"Touch me…"

He did as she asked, and her eyes closed in pleasure, her hands covering his as he skimmed over the velvet flesh of her stomach, her waist, then up over her ribs to finally cup her breasts. His thumbs teased her already sensitive nipples and she hissed, grinding harder into him.

She leaned down and he took her mouth in breathless kisses over and over, until he was about to explode, until the friction and heat where their bodies joined escalated to the point where they were both on the brink.

He felt her tighten around him and he groaned, gripping her hips and thrusting hard, until she panted against his mouth, her eyes squeezed shut. Then, with a soft cry and a ragged breath, he felt her go over the edge.

He shuddered, a deep, satisfied groan wrenching from his lips as he followed her. She collapsed on his chest as he murmured her name, his breath against her cheek, arms tight, holding her close. He felt her response against his neck, her body damp and shaking as she wrapped her arms around him, legs tightening with a sigh. "Don't move. Stay right here."

"I'm not going anywhere, *chérie*." His fingers went

into her hair, stroking her nape as the tight throb in his body began to slowly ease.

He blinked.

He loved her.

Just when the hell had that happened? And how? He searched his memory, going over each moment with determined concentration. Had it happened since that night ten weeks ago? Or sooner?

A frown furrowed his brow. It really didn't matter when, just that it *was*. He loved her as a best friend, as a lover. As a smart, amazing, funny, gorgeous and incredibly vulnerable woman. He loved that fourteen-year-old girl with the perfect hair and bright blue eyes, who'd stood up to his teasing. He loved that vulnerable, crazy nineteen-year-old, the one who'd needed him so desperately, the one who'd leaned on his shoulder, who'd needed *him* in her moment of grief. The woman who'd made mistakes in love and life and still continued to get back up, to forge her way and give the finger to all her critics.

The woman who had just received the worst possible news you could ever get.

No. He couldn't stop reality from intruding, but damn, he gave it his best shot. He knew the moment she felt it, too; her breath shook just a little on the intake and her arms tightened around him.

"No, don't," he said softly.

Too late.

She slowly slid off him in silence. As she fiddled with her underwear and pulled her skirt down, he took the moment to quickly adjust his pants. When he swung his feet to the floor, his breath snagged at her expression. How much effort was she exerting now, just to remain so calm, so in control? She was trying to hold it all together so he wouldn't see her at her absolute worst.

When she turned her back to him to do up her buttons, the curse he swallowed hurt like jagged glass. *Don't you dare lose it. Not when she's managing to keep it all together.*

"We should find out when we can go back to the mainland," he said softly, her back still to him. He had a few seconds to admire the smooth skin of her thighs, the gentle curve of her hip, the strong shoulders as she squared them and finally turned to face him, pushing back that mane of hair.

"Yes. I'll need to make some more calls, too."

"Kat." He leaned forward, looped an arm around her waist and pulled her to him. Surprisingly she offered no protest, just went into his arms silently. He held her, without passion and without subterfuge, just two friends sharing an embrace.

Finally he said, "Let's not jump to any conclusions here. They want to retest you. We should wait until that happens before we start making decisions."

He felt her nod against his chest, knew without confirmation that she was already thinking, planning. Making decisions. Her brain never stopped working, and now, of all days, she needed to make logical, sensible choices.

With a sigh she finally pulled away from him, and reluctantly he let her go. She went over to the table and grabbed her phone. "I have to make a few calls."

Seven

After Marco confirmed that the port at Cairns would reopen in a few hours, Kat used all her negotiation skills—and a few pleas—to wrangle an appointment with the geneticist for the very next day. Then they made a number of calls to let people know they were alive and well.

From what they gathered, Cairns was a disaster area. Parts of the city still had no water and electricity, and phone coverage was spotty. With the tropical climate, it was crucial those services be up and running again as soon as possible. It would be an arduous task, one that required a coordinated effort of all rescue services, plus private contractors. At least when the ports were clear and operating, supplies could be shipped in, and the massive cleanup could begin.

Armed with that information, they set about doing

physical tasks around the house—ripping the tape off the windows they hadn't already gotten to, and clearing more of the debris that would probably take a few weeks to get into some semblance of order, because all services would give priority to the mainland.

It was good to keep busy, to just focus on the pure physicality of lifting, clearing, moving. She'd assumed there'd be no time to think about tests, babies, Grace or the situation with Marco, but as they worked and sweat quickly soaked Kat's shirt, she found her mind was not so easily swayed.

You can't have this baby. She couldn't. It was the exact reason she'd vowed not to have kids. Her heart squeezed painfully and she scowled, putting more force than necessary into her raking task.

What her mother had gone through, what *she'd* gone through, watching her slowly wither and die from that death sentence… It was a pain so unfathomable that she'd willingly shift a mountain to prevent it from happening. It was one thing to cope with having the disease, to know exactly what she'd be facing every single day for the rest of her short life. But to willingly bring a child into that equation? No. Never.

Her eyes flicked briefly to Marco, then away. Yes, the pain of termination would cut deep, but it was preferable to a lifetime of anguish, of knowing she could have prevented it but selfishly did nothing. She would not put a child nor Marco through that.

Ah. No. Don't think about it. But she couldn't help it—her thoughts were already there, crowding her head with every single possible scenario until it was the only thing she could think about.

She gritted her teeth, wielding the rake with such

force that she heard the handle creak. *Damn. Something else. Think of...the cyclone. Work. Yes, work.* Grace would want her on top of this, sourcing stories, digging up information. She'd be so busy she wouldn't have a second to scratch herself, let alone think about...*that*.

She winced. And so it would begin again—Grace would choose the stories worthy of their effort and attention, the appropriate donation lines would be set up and a dozen other untold issues would remain just a couple of sentences in her notes.

The futility frustrated her.

And so she spent the next half hour focused on cleaning up, and eventually, with her arm and thigh muscles aching from the effort, they managed to clear a good part of the mess surrounding the house.

Finally Marco straightened, grabbed a bottle of water from beneath the tree and took a swig, then picked up his phone. "We should finish up."

Kat paused, scratching at a thin bead of sweat running down her neck as he handed her another bottle. "Okay."

"We'll probably make the mainland by three."

She nodded, one hand on her hip as she took a long swallow.

When he fell silent, she could feel his eyes on her. "Kat..."

Her gaze snapped to his as she finished the water, and the look in his eyes had her insides crumbling all over again. "Marco," she breathed. "Don't."

"But I have to say—"

"No," she said, a little too forcefully. "Don't say a thing. We did that already and look where that's gotten us. I don't want to say anything more until I have those follow-up tests in my hands. Until I know for sure." She studied him for a moment, taking in the tightness bracketing his mouth, his slightly clenched fist. "Promise me. No talk until we know."

As the seconds stretched, she held her breath, willing him with her mind. She'd coped with her mother's illness by not discussing, by not talking. She couldn't recall having one single deep and meaningful conversation with her father about what was going on, how she was coping, what he was feeling. He wasn't a talker at the best of times, but in this his lips had been perfectly sealed. Not talking was the only way she knew—that and partying until the nights had all just become one big, glitzy blur.

If Marco made her discuss just one more thing about this mind-boggling situation, she was sure she'd dissolve into a bawling mess on the floor.

"Fine."

Her breath whooshed out, relief flooding in. "Thank you. Now—" she attempted a smile but it fell way flat "—I don't know about you but I definitely need a shower before we head back to civilization."

How she managed to keep everything together for the entire day, Marco would never know. It was a testament to her inner strength, to her willpower, that she went through the motions of the boat trip strong and silently, pale-faced but determinedly swallowing her nausea.

And slowly, as the mainland came closer and closer, their attention was commanded by the shocking result of Cyclone Rory against the mainland of Cairns.

The radio reports had done nothing to prepare them for the devastation. It looked as if someone had stomped through in giant boots and created total havoc. A dozen private boats were all bunched up and shoved against the harbor wall like toys. The majestic palm trees were flattened, some crushing houses, some merely uprooted. Debris, sand, trees, glass, broken buildings and belongings... Everything had been displaced and reorganized into odd clusters, like the small speedboat half-buried in a luxury beach house. The kid's bike hanging from a lone palm tree. A cracked plasma TV lying in the middle of a now-sand-covered Esplanade pool. There were ripped roofs and scattered belongings and broken dreams left bare and torn.

Everywhere they looked, the cyclone had transformed the coastline into something neither of them recognized. In solemn silence they managed to dock, even though flotsam still floated in the water, then picked their way across the amazing wreck that was The Esplanade, to the next street, where Marco had arranged for a car to pick them up.

The drive north through town was made in similar silence as they were guided through the traffic snarl and stared out at the damage, trying to wrap their heads around the utter devastation the storm had wrought.

Physical devastation to accompany the emotional.

Marco swallowed, his gaze going briefly to Kat in the passenger seat, then back to the litter-strewn road, his eyes firmly on the police and rescue workers directing traffic and controlling the dozen news cars competing with business owners and volunteers eager to start the cleanup.

No, he had to stop those thoughts right now. They didn't know. Not until—as she said—she had the hard evidence in her hand. Then they would deal with whatever needed to be dealt with. So he bundled all those horrible thoughts, the possible future scenarios, and locked them up tight.

Her ringing phone provided some respite. After a brief conversation that mostly involved her listening to the caller, she hung up and said, "Grace needs me."

He simply nodded.

"I'll drop you off."

When they pulled up outside the studio, Kat swung from the car and then glanced back.

"Thanks. I'll let you know how I go."

"You sure you don't want me there?" he asked for the third time, studying her face carefully as she leaned in.

She nodded. "Grace confided in me. I should be the one to tell her. And the sooner she knows the better." Her ironic smile was brief. "Preempt that press statement I just know she's been working on."

He snorted but said nothing more, so she gave him a smile, said "Thanks" again and left.

But as she strode into the studio, her mind was still on the island, far from the Grace situation. It was as if the time they'd spent there had been their own personal bubble. Now it was back to reality.

She sighed as she dug out her ID and then swept into the building. Time to focus on what she needed to tell Grace.

"Just say whatever comes into your head" had been Marco's advice on the boat. And he was right. Some of her best stuff for *The Tribune* had been spontaneous and off-the-cuff. Too much rehearsing had felt overedited and scripted. This was one time where she didn't want things to sound forced.

With a pounding heart, she clipped down the corridor straight to her office, grabbing a runner on the way to determine Grace's whereabouts. She eventually ended up at the canteen, pausing in the doorway to scan the room, her eyes eventually landing on the TV star at a corner table with their executive producer.

Right. This was it. She took a deep breath and strode over, a smile on her face.

Grace spotted her a few feet away, and a second later she gasped and shot to her feet, commanding everyone's attention.

"Kat! Oh, my God, it's great to see you! How've you been?"

She was quickly enveloped in a warm Estee Lauder–scented hug, and then firmly cheek kissed. "You were so vague on the phone—you were with Marco on the island, right? Did the cyclone hit there or pass by? Was there much damage? Did you take photos? Sit and tell me everything!"

Acutely aware of the sudden attention, Kat went through the motions of nodding and smiling, accepting hugs and arm pats then thanking everyone for their good wishes until her face started to ache from the smiling. Finally, when the minor fuss had settled and everyone moved back to their tables, she leaned in to Grace.

"I need to talk to you. Privately."

Grace's unlined brow went up. "Sure. Let's go into my office."

It took a few minutes to get out of the canteen and then down the corridor. But finally they were in Grace's vibrant yellow-and-blue office, the air smelling faintly of Estee Lauder's Beautiful, her signature scent.

"So, what's up, Kat?" Grace smiled curiously, closing the door behind her. "Did you want to run a new story idea past me?"

"No." Kat eased onto the edge of the sofa, her insides churning. "It's about Marco."

"Oh?"

"Yes." Boy, this was awkward, way more awkward than she'd thought. It was because it was Grace, someone she cared about. Someone who'd be hurt, no matter how skillful or pretty or unscripted her words were. It was personal this time, and she hated every single minute of it.

Still, she had to put on her big-girl knickers and get it done. So she took a breath and plunged right in.

"Grace. Marco and me…me and him… Well, we're kind of…" Kind of what? *Together? Bed partners? Having a baby?* "Involved," she finished lamely.

Oh, way to go. Put those media skills to great use there.

Silence reigned, somehow made thicker by the soft fragrance permeating the air, as the expression on Grace's perfectly made-up face went through the emotions in a matter of seconds—amused surprise, confusion, disbelief—until she settled on a dark frown. "I'm sorry…what?"

"Marco and I are…involved."

Grace slowly crossed her arms. "Yes, you said that. But what does that actually mean? You guys are always involved in one way or another."

"We slept together."

Grace's eyes rounded. "What? When?"

Kat swallowed, her gaze firm. "Ten weeks ago, just before he left for France." *And these past few days…* Although she didn't need to spell that out, because judging from the look on Grace's face, she'd already assumed that.

Grace's slow blink and sudden laden silence said everything and yet nothing at all. So instead of elaborating, instead of trying to justify an action that had obviously cut deep, Kat waited.

Grace slowly sat down behind her desk then leaned back on the plush office chair, her face carefully blank. "I see. A little farewell private party, was it?"

"Grace…" Kat's chest tightened. God, this was hard! "You two weren't together at the time—"

"Oh, thanks for checking on that." The brief grimace slashing Grace's features twisted a little knife in Kat's belly. "It makes me feel so much better."

"I meant, I didn't plan on—"

Grace held up a hand. "Stop. I really don't need to know the details." She paused, raking her gaze over Kat until the burn of humiliation and betrayal had formed a small pool of sweat at the base of her spine.

"You knew when I mentioned wanting a baby," Grace finally said.

Kat nodded.

"And you said nothing."

Kat nodded again. "And I'm really sorry about that. I didn't know what to say. At that point, the thing with me and Marco was just a…a…one-time thing. We'd both decided to just ignore it and move on. But now, after these last few days, we've talked and it's all become a bit more…um…complicated."

"How?"

Kat flushed. "Just…complicated."

Grace's eyes narrowed. "You're not pregnant, are you?"

The shock of having it put right out there made Kat gasp, and she had to scramble for a breath. "Wh—what?"

"Are you pregnant?" Grace repeated, her expression tight.

Because it was Grace, a person she admired and respected, a person she'd come to trust with parts of her personal life, Kat hesitated over her automatic denial. But it was the small hesitation that gave it away, gave Grace clear and direct confirmation. And when the older woman's face creased into a small smile, Kat's conflict grew a thousandfold.

Please don't ask. I can barely wrap my head around it all myself...and the test results just totally screw everything up.

Kat bit her lip and slid her gaze away. "No comment."

Silence descended for a few moments, silence in which Kat firmly swallowed every emotion she'd been battling the past day. Damn, she couldn't lose it again. She *wouldn't* lose it again. She'd had her moment of weakness with Marco, had let the overwhelming feelings command her, make her vulnerable. She couldn't do it every single time someone mentioned it. Otherwise she'd just be a blubbering wreck on the floor.

Grace finally sighed and said, "I can't deny I'm hurt, Kat."

She grimaced. "I know. And I am really, really sorry about that. But it wasn't planned. If there's anything I can do to make it right for you…"

"An interview."

Kat blinked, her brow furrowed. "What?"

"You can give me that interview we were talking

about." Grace stood swiftly, hands wide on her desk, a gleam in her eye.

Oh, wow. That was a bit... Kat's head spun a little. "That's...uh. No."

"You're still saying no?" Grace lifted her brow. "After what you've just told me? Knowing nothing in this business is kept a secret for long?" At Kat's look of alarm, she waved a hand in the air. "Oh, honey, you should know by now it won't be me leaking details to the press. But once others get involved, it's inevitable."

Kat remained silent as Grace gave her a long look, then fished out a makeup bag from her desk and went through the motions of reapplying lipstick. It was true. A secret was kept only by one person, and over the next few days more and more people would be involved, like it or not.

"The offer is still there," Grace finally said, unplugging her phone and scrolling through her messages. "We'd do it your way, with your final approval. And you know I don't often say that."

Kat paused, trying to get everything straight in her head. "So you're okay with the Marco thing?"

"No." Grace smiled thinly.

She swallowed. "Grace...is this going to be awkward between us?"

"Most likely." The older woman eyed her, her expression still tight. "You denied it too much, you know. I always knew you had a thing—one that predates my claim—so I shouldn't be that surprised."

Kat swallowed her guilt, glancing away. "That's not what—"

"Oh, please." Grace rolled her eyes theatrically as she

walked to the door and pulled it open. "Give me some credit here. You and Marco have *always* been a thing."

Kat followed her out the door then down the corridor in silence, until Grace finally turned and eyed her. "So when are you going public?"

"*If,* Grace," Kat said. "If we go public."

Grace threw her a knowing look over her shoulder. "Oh, it's a 'when,' hon. Trust me."

Kat frowned. "That's not something we've thought about."

"Really?" Grace kept walking. "Well, you'd better start. Gossip has a way of getting out, you know."

Kat stared at her back. Was that a threat? That definitely sounded like one. And to be honest, she couldn't deny Grace her bitterness. If she could make this right with her, she'd gladly do it.

Even giving her an exclusive?

Ugh. That thought lay heavy in her gut for the rest of the afternoon, until she finally made her way home, barely made it through a shower and finally collapsed into a blissful sleep coma on her bed.

Eight

The next day Marco and Kat sat in Dr. Hardy's waiting room, nervously waiting for her name to be called. Most structures in North Cairns had survived cyclone damage and it was still a surreal sight to see: half the town had been flattened while the other half stood tall and proud as if everything was normal.

Instead of offering empty it'll-be-okays and you'll-be-all-rights, he remained silent, loosely holding her hand, occasionally brushing her knuckles with his thumb as the minutes ticked by.

One minute.

Five.

Ten.

He glanced at the clock then scanned the pristine waiting room for the umpteenth time. Life still went on, despite the destruction outside. People still needed results, still needed diagnosing, needed to know what was wrong and how to fix it. Only a few people waited with them—a young couple, an elderly man, a woman with two small children—and briefly he wondered what each of their stories was, how they'd come to be here, right now. How they would cope with bad news, what they had vowed to change if the prognosis was good.

He watched the young mother settle her toddler with a book, and he smiled at her as their eyes met over the child's head.

That could be Kat in a few years' time.

Or not.

"Thank you for coming with me," she said now with a small smile.

"I wouldn't be anywhere else, *chérie*." He squeezed her hand, careful to keep his worry firmly under wraps as he met her gaze. She needed him to be strong, whatever the result. He was there as her best friend, not the man who loved her so much he'd willingly sell his soul to trade places if he could.

Her finger softly traced his frown lines with a half smile. "Don't," she said softly.

He captured her hand, kissed it gently before his gaze slid away. "Sorry."

"Please, Marco. I really couldn't cope if you fell apart on me now."

He nodded, breath catching for a moment before he slowly huffed it out.

You need to tell her.

He grimaced, his gaze firmly on the floor. *No.* She had told him quite firmly they were friends. Nothing more. He had no doubt if he did tell her, that it would be the end of their friendship. And fighting about that now, proving to her that they should be together when she had so much more on her mind, would take everything he had. Waiting was not something he did well, but he wanted her in his life. He'd damn well have to wait for now, regardless of how it frustrated him.

Just not for long.

The door suddenly opened and all eyes went to Dr. Hardy as he walked purposefully over to them with a pleasant smile.

His heart thudded, hard.

"Good afternoon, Kat. Thanks for coming in." He said it softly, but still the people closest to them heard. A gentle murmur of recognition rippled, followed by all eyes swiveling to her as she stood with a flush. To her credit she ignored it all, just tightened her hand in Marco's and followed the doctor down the hall.

"Have you seen the town?" Dr. Hardy began as they settled in his office, his elderly face creased into concerned lines.

"Yes. It's unbelievable."

"Not quite as bad as Yasi but pretty grim."

She nodded, her expression neutral. Yeah, she was impatient, though. Marco could tell by the small muscles bracketing her mouth, the slight dip of her eyebrows.

"So," Marco said. "The tests. You ran them again?"

"We did." Dr. Hardy coughed then slowly removed his glasses, tossing them on the file.

"And?"

He spent interminable seconds shuffling through the file, then finally pulled out a piece of paper and read, pausing way too long.

Kat leaned in with a frown. "What?"

Dr. Hardy flushed. "First, I want to offer you my heartfelt sympathies for what you've been going through. We do have strict protocols, and regretfully I broke from that because of the history I had with your mother." He coughed. "But right now I can confirm that…" He stared at the paper before returning to her. "There was a mix-up at the lab. Some samples were mislabeled. And as a result, you have tested negative for motor neuron disease."

It was like taking a football to the chest, meted out by the world's best striker. Marco's gasp mingled with Kat's softer, higher one. Her hand went still in his as she froze, eyes wide. Her voice, when it came, wavered as if she'd just raced up a flight of stairs. "I'm sorry…what?"

"Your blood-test results have tested negative for motor neuron disease. You are clear and healthy, and—"

Marco's pounding heart drowned out the rest. She was healthy. The tests were clear.

The relief was unlike anything he'd ever known in his life. Nothing compared—not national selection, not the not-guilty verdict from his father's trial. Not even the positive results after his knee surgery telling him that yes, he would be able to walk. This…oh, this…

Joy, pure unadulterated joy choked his breath, and he felt the crazy laugh well inside, just before he choked it down.

She's going to have a child. Our child.

His expletive came out like a shot, and then he was turning to her and dragging her into a hug that was way too tight, way too emotional, but damn, she was clear, and the joy that swelled was too hard to contain.

She was going to live to see their child grow up. Take its first steps. Go to school, go on dates, get married.

Damn, she was going to *live*.

Eventually he pulled back enough to cup her teary face, knowing his smile stretched from ear to ear, because hers matched it.

"Clear," she whispered, her joyful expression a watery mess.

"Clear," he repeated, then slowly added, "We're going to have a baby."

Her eyes widened for a second, and then a small nod followed. "Oh, we so are."

Kat swallowed. She had tested negative. She was having a baby.

She couldn't even begin to quantify these two life-changing statements. She'd done enough survivor stories to know the emotion involved in processing this kind of information. The mix of elation and sheer panic running through her mind right now was…overwhelming. Overpowering. It choked her breath, snagged a laugh in her throat, forced tears to her eyes.

She stared at Marco as he brushed her damp cheeks with a shaky hand. How many times had she nodded sympathetically when all those survivors had tried to verbalize their feelings, tried to compose their thoughts into some semblance of control yet let everyone know of the emotion behind it? But she didn't know, not really.

Until now.

The adrenaline rush was amazing. She wanted to cry and laugh and dance and take on the world. She wanted to do reckless things just for the hell of it. She wanted to fulfill all those silly, crazy dreams she and Marco had laughingly thought up in ninth grade, trying to outdo each other on the ridiculous scale. Bungee jumping off the Eiffel Tower. Hiring Disneyland for the day. Biking down Everest. Flying a fighter jet.

She wanted to *live*.

After all these years of steadfastly refusing to get tested, pushing the worry and doubt to the back of her mind, then those agonizing hours of unbelievable anguish, she had finally been cut a break.

Everything seemed surreal, as if she was walking through a dream where nothing and no one could touch her. And couple that with Marco's gentle kiss, his obvious joy at her results, and there was no better moment than this, right here.

It was… Well, she couldn't even find the words to describe it. *Amazing* and *unbelievable* were way too tame for such a life-changing occasion.

She wasn't sick.

Dr. Hardy's discreet cough, when it came, had them both turning in surprise. He sat in the same position, leaning forward on the desk, arms bent, his expression professional.

"Thanks, Doctor," Kat got out, the smile stretching her face until it ached. "That's the best news I could've had."

"You're welcome." He leaned back in his chair, a hand brushing over his sparse gray hair. "There is, however, one more issue."

"Yes?"

He cleared his throat and focused his gaze on her. "Your mother's blood group is O, correct?"

She nodded. "Yes, it was in the hospital documents."

"And you are AB."

"Yes."

"Well, here's our problem."

She shook her head. "Sorry, I'm not getting it."

"Kat, normally I'd recommend further blood tests, make the standard speech about getting more results, seeing your doctor, etc., etc. But I knew your mother for a long time and I owe you this." He sighed. "I'm saying an O parent cannot have an AB child."

She blinked then shook her head with a snort. "Well, obviously there's been a mistake. We need to test it again."

He fixed her with a look, part sympathy, part concern. "I'm sorry. It's been done three times already. There's no mistake."

What?

Kat stilled, her thoughts all crammed in tight as she tried to decipher what this meant.

Okay, so her mother was O. She was AB. And O and AB couldn't be related. Which meant...

Her hand suddenly tightened in Marco's. "Hang on, you're saying it's impossible for my mother to be my *mother?*"

Dr. Hardy nodded.

"No," she croaked, and then more firmly said, "No, the tests are wrong. Just...just..." she stammered, her head whirling. "Just like with my first results! An accident. Human error."

"No, it's quite correct. We were very careful this time around. Everything was done properly." He paused, taking in her pale face and thinning mouth. "Kat, look, I can put you in touch with someone who—"

She stood so quickly, the blood rushed to her head. "I can't...I can't..." She didn't finish that sentence, just strode over to the door and stalked out.

Impossible. Ridiculous. It had to be a mistake.

She made it out the waiting room, then down the corridor, oblivious to Marco calling her. The elevators gave her pause, and she viciously punched an elevator button as her mind tried to make sense of these past few days, put them in neat little boxes and bring her some order and peace.

She couldn't. She was as far from peace as she could possibly be right now. She'd had a life-threatening disease for a day and everything involved in that—the feelings, the worry, the entire universe of emotion that came with the ordeal—had drained her. Yes, she'd managed to wrap her head around it, even though part of her deep down had refused to accept it. And now here she was, her greatest wish come true. She was disease-free....

But she had no clue who she was.

Who was her real mother? Was her father even her father? Did she have brothers, sisters out there somewhere? Where was she born? Did she look like anyone in her family?

Had someone given her up and then turned around and walked away without another thought? Was she stolen? Or had her parents loved her and been involved in some horrible accident?

A sob caught in her throat and she lifted a shaky hand to her mouth, determinedly glaring at the elevator doors as she felt the tears form.

It was as if someone had just suddenly erased her entire past, every single moment and memory effectively wiped and replaced with...what?

A million questions.

She sensed rather than saw Marco standing beside her, a silent presence that did little to calm her chaotic insides.

Was her real name Katerina, or was that another lie? Did her father know? Did *anyone* know?

Just who the *hell* was she?

She choked back a sob just when the elevator doors swung open, and she silently entered, hand still on her mouth as if to hold in all those raw, spilling emotions.

Marco pressed the basement-floor button and finally broke the silence. "What are you going to do?"

Her eyes remained firmly on the doors as she desperately tried to gain control, swallowing thickly and blinking over and over. She would not break down here, not now.

Later, yes. Not here.

"I'm going to see my dad."

A pause. "Flights will be limited until the airport's given the all clear."

"I know. I'll take the next available to Brisbane."

"I'll come with you."

Desperate for something else to focus on, she pulled out her phone and tapped on the travel app. "You don't have to do that."

"I want to."

"Can you take time off work?"

"I'll make time," he said firmly. "This is important."

She chanced a glance at his determined expression and then quickly looked away. *Of course you want him there.*

Just as during every other emotional time in her life, his presence would give her the necessary strength to get through this. He was her first and last choice.

"Okay. I'll let you know." The elevator opened and she walked out the foyer, then through the automatic doors. "Can you drop me off home?"

"Sure."

They walked across the car park to the vehicle in silence, and when she finally slid onto the soft leather seat with a groan, she closed her eyes. She was physically and emotionally drained. Thank God Marco said nothing, just drove in silence.

They finally reached her apartment block, and still not a word had been said.

What could she possibly say? She'd been through the emotional wringer and her brain was desperate to focus on something else. Yet when she crawled out of the car and glanced back at him, the small frown furrowing his brow and the look on his face crumbled her composure. "Kat, are you okay?"

She gave him a shaky smile. "No, actually. But I will be."

"Do you want me to come up?"

She pulled back, shaking her head. "No. No, thanks. I just need some time alone. Time to sort some things out."

"Okay." His blatant skepticism almost had her smiling. Almost.

"I'll call you." With that she turned and walked off, her disappointment echoing with every click of her heels on concrete.

What was she expecting? She'd said no, and he'd taken her at her word. End of discussion.

Except her reality had been ripped from her in the space of one afternoon, and she had no idea what to think or feel anymore. So instead of focusing on the whole messed-up bag of her parentage—the sensible thing when she had no clear answers—she latched on to the other issue she'd been avoiding.

Her and Marco.

Marco's reality was being absent six months out of the year. And the truth was, she didn't want him 30, 50, even 80 percent of his time. She needed his 100 percent commitment. But she also knew she couldn't ask that of him.

She unlocked the door to her third-floor apartment and went in, tossing her bag onto the kitchen counter and yanking open the fridge.

Honestly, it'd be easier for both of them if she raised this child by herself.

She could do that. She'd take time off work, hire a nanny. Women did it all the time, and she was in the fortunate position of having a healthy bank account to ease the burden.

And yet...

Hadn't she always resented her parents' piecemeal approach to parenting? Oh, her mother had been there when she could, but she'd been so involved in her work as an exclusive events planner she'd missed the bulk of Kat's high school activities. And her father... Well, she had as much chance of flying the starship *Enterprise* as she had of seeing him there for her. It would've been a shock to actually have her father attend something.

Their long and pointed absences had hurt the most, the overwhelming feeling that they'd just simply lost interest, gotten bored or had something more important to focus on shaping her insecurity all the way through high school. The familiar thread of instability still made her gut tighten even now.

Except she wasn't her mother's daughter, was she? Maybe they hadn't been totally committed because the blood bond that tied normal families together wasn't there. Maybe she was a disappointment, someone they'd not come to expect much of. And when her mother had become sick—

A sudden sickening realization swept over her, and she grabbed the bench for support.

If Nina wasn't her biological mother, and they'd known all along…

Then they'd know she wasn't a carrier or infected.

They had *known*. And not told her. For nearly fourteen years, her father had had so many opportunities to reveal this information, to put her mind at rest. But he hadn't. He'd let her go on believing every single day that her body was a ticking time bomb and that she could fall sick at any time.

The cry that erupted from her throat was almost primeval. She actually felt physically sick.

How on earth could the secret of her birth be more important than her physical and mental health?

Her hand shook as she poured a glass of juice and then quickly placed the carton on the bench. Her head hurt just trying to sort through everything. She could either make herself crazy going around in circles about it, or she could do something. Except until she saw her father, there was nothing *to* do.

Wrong. She could start to preempt the damage.

She grabbed her phone from the bench and scrolled through the contacts, finally calling a Brisbane number she'd never thought she'd need again—the publicist who'd skillfully navigated her around her last disastrous divorce, then those awful photos.

"Emma?" she said when the woman picked up. "It's Kat Jackson. I need to hire you."

Nine

Three days later, after Kat had begged off early on Friday afternoon, she and Marco managed to get a flight into Brisbane, and Kat arranged to meet her father at work during his lunch hour. Not that he actually took one, she thought, as they both rode the elevator up to the executive offices of Jackson & Blair International Investments. She'd grown up on the stories of how her father and Stephen Blair had overcome the odds of humble family beginnings to develop their business. How they'd used their trademark determination and ruthlessness to throw every penny and waking moment into what was now one of Australia's top-ten investment companies.

And with such a sacrifice came a price. She barely remembered her father during her childhood. Instead he stood out by his lengthy absences—the times her mother had brought her to the offices for their "quality time," the weekends vying for his attention when he'd been on the phone, in his office or hunched over some important papers. In that, she and Connor had bonded, recognizing similar upbringings but rarely needing words to confirm it.

If Keith Jackson had intimidated her growing up, Stephen Blair had done so tenfold. Even now, passing by his office on their way to her father's, catching a bare glimpse of his towering, expensively suited presence in heavy discussion with similarly suited men, was enough to set her nerves on edge. He was a man who silently judged, for whom perfection meant everything, and nothing was good enough unless it was his way.

What a nightmare for Connor to have a father like that.

Five minutes later, Kat left Marco in the waiting room and strode into her father's office, a mix of anger, intimidation and frustration congealing in her belly.

Calm. Stay calm. She had the truth on her side, and she had the courage to confront him because what he did was wrong.

"Katerina," Keith Jackson said with a thin smile as she walked into his office then closed the door behind her. "I'm surprised the network let you go amidst all the cyclone coverage."

"It's only one afternoon." Not to Grace it wasn't, and she had the feeling her boss would be calling in the favor fairly soon.

"So, what's so urgent you had to fly down to Brisbane to talk to me?"

She took a seat opposite him, saying nothing. On

the two-hour flight south, she'd rehearsed this over and over, until her head spun and she'd exhausted herself.

It simply wasn't possible for her father *not* to know. Which meant beyond a shadow of a doubt that he also knew the chances of her having her mother's disease were low to none.

He could have told her anytime. They both could have told her. Instead they'd said absolutely nothing, letting her go through the pain, the anguish, then the ultimate decision to not get tested. Anger had surged every time she thought about that, so she'd vowed to not think about it until she had confirmation. Then she could silently go to pieces.

"I need to ask you something and I need you to tell me the truth, okay?"

His eyebrows went up, mouth in an impatient "okay" expression, as if she'd just told him she was buying a new handbag or going to the Gold Coast for the weekend.

"Dad," she said without preamble, her gaze direct. "Am I adopted?"

His expression froze, a perfect display of shock and confusion all rolled into one. She waited calmly as he leaned back in his chair with a dark frown, his face faintly flushed.

"What kind of question is that?" he said tightly.

"A perfectly legitimate one, considering it's impossible for Mum's blood type, O, to produce a child of my AB type."

His long pause was telling. "And why on earth are you getting blood tests? I thought you didn't want to know."

"I'm pregnant, Dad." Wow, that came out way smoother

than she'd practiced. It felt liberating, actually. "And I wanted to know if I had the disease. I don't, by the way. But then, you probably already knew that, considering Mum isn't really my mother."

She'd never seen him so still. Wow, she'd actually robbed him of speech—an ironic first. Swallowing the hysterical little laugh, she just slowly folded her arms and stared at him. And yet, he said nothing.

Great. It was up to her, then.

"Did you have an affair? Did the woman leave you with the baby?"

"No!" He flushed again, this time deeper. "That's ridiculous."

"So I'm adopted."

His nod, when it came, was frustratingly short.

She clamped down hard on her anger, but it still ended up bubbling over. "Oh, my God, Dad! I've had that disease hanging over my head for *years,* sitting there in the back of my mind, a death sentence." She sprung to her feet, fury flushing her face hot. "How the *hell* can you justify not telling me? Why on earth would you let me go through all those years of worry, of thinking…of thinking…" She couldn't stand there and finish the sentence, not with her father's face twisted into such uncharacteristic lines of pain that it hurt her heart just to look at him.

It was like the night of her mother's death, the only time she'd ever seen him weak and vulnerable, a man without power, without control. Just a man.

It had scared the hell out of her. Just as it did now.

She slowly sat, hands gripped on the armrests. "So why adopt? And why keep it a secret?" Her gaze softened. "Dad, if Mum couldn't have kids, it's nothing to be ashamed of. Why didn't you just tell me?"

He sighed, leaning back in his chair. "Because we made a promise."

"To whom?"

When he shook his head, her irritation spiked again. "Dad, tell me!"

He scowled. "Why bring this up now, Kat? Don't you have other things to worry about—like how the press is going to react to you being pregnant?"

She blinked and bit back a curse. *That* was what he was worried about? "I'm handling that."

His expression was borderline skeptical. "Right."

Dark, hot anger surged, making her skin tingle with the power of it, but her voice was calm, unwavering. "We're talking about my blood tests, Dad."

Oh, she desperately wanted to spill the entire story of the past few days, throw the false positive in his face and reveal her anguish, anger and every other single emotion that had accompanied it. She even choked on a sob as the words caught in her throat, but at the very last minute she clenched her fists and bit her tongue.

He lapsed into silence again, and she just stared at him. She knew her face reflected all the thoughts and emotions bubbling to the surface, every single one of them. When he broke eye contact first, she took just a little joy in that.

"Your mother wanted to tell you, you know," he said, carefully moving his coffee cup from the corner of the desk to the middle. "Many times."

"Why didn't she?"

He sighed. "The timing was never quite right. Because she knew you'd start asking questions, and she couldn't answer any of them." He slid her a glance. "That was why we never pushed you to get tested. The likelihood of you being positive was practically non-existent."

She swallowed, dragged in a shaky breath as the past few days crashed over her. *You're negative. The test was negative, remember?* "Who are my birth parents?"

He paused a moment. "I can't tell you. I gave my word."

"Who on earth would make you promise something like that? Who would hold either so much power or so much loyalty...that...that..." She petered out, her mind clicking through the possibilities until she finally latched on to something crazy, something so far-fetched that she realized it fit perfectly.

No. It couldn't be *him*.

And yet...

It so totally could.

But that would mean...

Her back straightened in the chair. "It's Stephen Blair, isn't it?"

"No," he snapped quickly, the tight lines bracketing his mouth deepening.

It was so quick she barely had time to register it—the tiny twitch of a muscle near his eye, the clench of his hand. The almost imperceptible thinning of his lips. All signs of guilt.

"It so is." She stood, head spinning. "And I'm going to ask him."

"You will not!"

Her father's harsh command stopped her midturn. Slowly she turned back to face him, and his expression—

a mix of fury, tension and...yes, fear—was enough to temper her anger.

"Tell me, Dad," she said softly. "Please."

He paused, pursing his lips. She could practically see his brain working through the different outcomes of telling versus silence.

Thankfully, he made his decision quickly. "You can't say anything. Not even to Connor."

She blinked, gripping the chair back for support as the implication suddenly sank in. *Oh, God. Connor was...*

Connor was her *brother.* This was...

She couldn't even wrap her head around this. Connor. Her brother. Stephen. Her father. So...

"Who's my mother?"

He sighed then nodded to the chair. "Sit."

Marco sat in the waiting room, flicking through his phone and resisting the urge to get up and pace. For the fifth time he glanced up at the receptionist, and just as she had those five times before, she quickly dropped her gaze and hurriedly pretended to be doing something else.

Finally he strode over to the huge twentieth-floor window, to the panoramic view of Brisbane spread before him.

He sighed. When Kat was growing up, Keith Jackson had been the quintessential workaholic, but where he was gruff, terse and had little time for people other than his social circle, Kat's mother, Nina, had been his polar opposite. Whenever Kat talked about her mother, her face lit up, her eyes alight with love, even though she hadn't been a perfect parent herself. Marco had lost count of how many times he'd watched Kat swallow disappointment over her mother's prior commitments and broken promises. Yet all of that had become unimportant in the wake of her illness. And boy, he clearly remembered the time Kat had turned up on his doorstep in France, barely a few weeks after her mother had died. It was as if something essential had been stolen, something he wasn't sure she'd get back. But slowly, over time, she'd found her way back to who she was—his Kat. Changed, with added maturity, yes. But still Kat, deep down.

"I'm sorry, but aren't you Marco Corelli?"

His thoughts scattered, and as he glanced up at the receptionist, he quickly put on an automatic polite smile. "I am."

Her grin widened. "I knew it! My little brother plays local league and watches the European games religiously on cable. He's so excited for the World Cup selection next year, I can't tell you." She laughed. "He'll be so jealous I got to meet you."

Marco couldn't help but return her smile. "Thanks. We're all pretty excited about the selection, too."

"So will you be calling the match again? Our whole neighborhood stops to watch, you know," she added, rising from her seat, clutching pen and paper.

"That's the plan." When he held out his hand, she shook it in silent awe, and for the next few minutes, he answered her breathless questions, signed an autograph and smiled for a photo.

"Congratulations on the FFA award, by the way," she said, finally returning to her seat as the phone began to ring. "My cousins in Sydney will be stalking the red carpet on the night." She paused and picked up the handset with a smirk. "I'll have to text them that photo and make them jealous. Good morning, Jackson & Blair. How may I help you?"

"Marco?"

His soft laugh abruptly cut off and he whirled at the sound of Kat's voice, her pale face choking off the last of his amusement. He said nothing, just pushed the doors open for her, sent the receptionist a smile and a wave and followed Kat to the elevators.

"Well?" he asked as they rode down to the ground floor. "What did he say?"

She opened her mouth once, then closed it, then just stared at him, a dumbfounded expression on her face.

He gently took her shoulders. "Kat?"

"I am…" She shook her head, as if she couldn't believe it. "My father is…"

"Yes?"

She dragged in a harsh breath. "My birth father is Stephen Blair. Connor is my half brother."

His soft expletive bounced off the walls, but she barely winced, just turned back to the elevator doors, staring as the descending floor numbers lit up.

"Apparently Stephen had an affair with his housekeeper's daughter and I was the result." Her mouth thinned. "This was after my mum discovered she had motor neuron and decided not to have kids."

"And where's the housekeeper now?"

"They paid her off and she moved back to New Zealand. She died a few years ago."

He scowled.

"So they adopted you? Why keep it a secret? And how?"

"They went to the States for a year to hide the fact

my mother couldn't get pregnant." She sighed. "Stephen begged my father not to say anything—gave him the whole 'my wife will divorce me, my life will be ruined, the company will suffer' spiel. Dad agreed."

"And your dad just told you this voluntarily."

"Well, not at first." Her mouth thinned.

He paused, digesting that information.

"So are you going to tell Connor?"

The doors slid open and they walked through the elegant marble and crystal ground floor. "If you were him, would you want to know?"

He nodded. "Yes, I would. What about Stephen? Are you going to tell him you know?"

She remained silent as they pushed through the turnstile doors out onto George Street.

"I don't know." Her expression tightened. "I think it's a fair bet to say he won't care."

"Yeah." He glanced around then leaned in. "Whatever you decide, if you tell Connor—things always have a way of getting out." At her look, he added, "I'm not saying any of us would deliberately say anything. But the more people who know, the higher the chances."

She nodded then cast a casual glance up then down the busy Brisbane street, scanning the people going about their day. He noticed one or two do a double take as they passed, and he knew it was Kat they recognized and not him. The pull of her celebrity still amazed him, even after nearly a year of absence from the headlines.

Except that would soon end, and in spectacular fashion. His network had already fielded a handful of calls about his whereabouts during the cyclone, and he knew Kat had hired a publicist to issue a statement. Plus there was that thing with Grace, who was still on her case about an exclusive. After she announced her pregnancy, the press would start to piece things together, and then the nightmare would really start.

He suppressed a groan, remembering what it had been like the last time for her. All that stress, all that anxiety. Outwardly she'd handled it with aplomb, but he knew firsthand how much damage it had caused on the inside to her confidence, her self-esteem.

Not good for the baby.

They walked into the parking station, paid for the ticket and then made their way to his car, both wrapped up in their own thoughts until he glanced at his watch. Three hours before their flight.

With a frown he turned to face her, leaning against the door.

"Kat."

"Marco," she said in the same serious tone. God, he'd missed her humor. These past few days had drained him to the point that he wondered if things would ever get back to normal again.

He just wanted to see her smile again. Was that too much to ask?

"You don't have to do this, you know. You could just issue a statement then move into my place for a few weeks, until it blows over."

She stared at him for a moment and then slowly shook her head. "I have a job, Marco."

"One that Grace is making very difficult, so you said."

"She's angry. I understand that."

He let out a breath. "So if you're not going to take my suggestion or give Grace her exclusive, then tell me again why getting married would be a bad thing?"

Her expression twisted, telling him it was precisely the wrong thing to say. "Marco, please…"

He sighed. "Look, I'm trying to wrap my head around this and work out the best way to deal with everything."

"And you think I'm not?" She scowled. "My head is a mess. My life is…crazy. And my past, everything I just assumed was real? Gone. All thirty-three years of it." She slashed her eyes away from him, her frustration palpable. "Asking me to marry you is—"

An audible gasp interrupted her, and they both whirled to find two girls, shopping bags forgotten at their feet, busily clicking away with their cell phones.

One of them jiggled on the spot, a wide grin on her face. "Ohmygod, are you guys getting *married?* That is so awesome!"

Click, click, click.

Marco flushed, his hand instinctively going up to shield his face as he glanced to Kat, but she'd already moved and was yanking open the car door. She scrambled inside a moment later, and after he quickly joined her, he fired up the engine and they pulled out of the car park.

Her soft curse in the still air said it all, as did her glare in the rearview mirror. "That was—"

"Probably nothing," he said, taking the next turn to get them onto the highway. "A couple of fans."

"A couple of fans with cell phones and social media at their disposal," she muttered, glaring out the window, her face tight with emotion. Just as during the times before, he knew exactly what she was thinking.

Here we go again.

The phone calls, the questions, the borderline stalking. Her family getting hassled. Photographers camped on her doorstep, at work, at the gym. TV and radio dissecting and analyzing their every move, offering expert damage control.

And there wasn't a damn thing he could do about it.

"Kat…" he said now, but she quickly held up a hand and made a call.

"The press statement will be out today, for whatever good that'll do me," she said when she hung up.

"Maybe it's not that bad."

She gave him an "Oh, really?" look. "Trust me, something will show up."

He couldn't argue with that.

They drove another twenty minutes in silence, until they finally pulled into the airport parking station and Marco turned to her.

"I have to be in Darwin tomorrow," he said.

She glanced from the window to meet his eyes. "Oh?"

He nodded. "One of the remote coaching clinics I set up. We're doing a grand opening with the mayor."

"When are you back?"

"In a few days. I fly in Monday."

She nodded. "Okay."

"Listen, Kat, I don't want to leave you in the middle of this, but I also have a thing in Melbourne, then Sydney. I won't be back until the day before the FFA awards."

She shrugged. "It's okay."

"No, it's not." Her cavalier attitude irritated him—as if she expected his absence.

"I have an appointment for an ultrasound next week," she added.

Damn. He scowled. "Why didn't you tell me?"

"I'm telling you now."

He frowned. "I could've rescheduled."

She gave him a look. "Not when you're booked months in advance. And anyway, it's only an ultrasound."

He dragged a hand through his hair. "I'm not abandoning you, Kat."

"I know. But until I make a public announcement, I think we should keep you out of it, don't you?"

He gritted his teeth and grabbed the handle, swinging the door wide. "No, I bloody well don't. Honestly, this is getting ridiculous. There comes a time when you just have to say, 'What the hell,' ignore what everyone says about you and live your life."

He got out of the car, slammed the door and, with long-legged strides, headed into the airport terminal, Kat following. And thanks to that little encounter earlier, he spent the whole time surreptitiously glancing around at the crowd, wondering if someone somewhere was taking photos, eavesdropping on their conversation. It was bloody unnerving.

Finally they made it through departures, past the check-in counter and into Qantas's private VIP lounge, which consisted of a bar, dining area, plush lounges and a communications center. They settled in and ordered drinks and food, but otherwise the silence stretched out between them. Marco checked his phone. Kat opened her iPad for her mail. Still not a word.

Was this how a friendship ended? he thought as he stared at his phone screen. Not with a spectacular all-out screaming match, but in a forced silence so uncomfortable she couldn't even bring herself to look at him.

It wasn't an argument. They didn't hate each other. He just… She just…

She didn't want to marry him. And he wanted her to.

He scowled at his phone. They had nineteen years between them, and he was damned if he'd let her push him out of her life. Once they dealt with this current situation, they'd have a serious talk about everything—including marriage.

It must've been some kind of record. Barely a day later, their "marriage proposal" hit social media, then the national papers, spreading out what could have just been a one-off article into a planned series on celebrity weddings and divorces, which were advertised with annoying regularity on TV. Marco and Kat were, of course, given plenty of airtime through the media, and, with the tabloid press, including the TV networks, setting up camp at her home, she'd had to hire a driver to take her to and from work.

Some photos still managed to leak out—one of her getting out of the car at the station. One when she'd not quite closed her curtains all the way. And some old cringe-worthy celebrity shots of her in full party mode.

That last one had been published two days ago, and she hadn't heard from Marco since. A dozen times she'd picked up the phone, ready to call, but stopped herself every time. It was something they needed to talk about face-to-face, not get into over the phone.

Of course, Grace had been mega-pissed about the attention, and the pressure at work had been high, compounding her stress about her family issues. After each day of her Job from Hell, she'd come home and collapsed on the sofa, finally allowing herself to think about the whole adoption thing, not to mention where to start finding out if her biological mother had had family, which in turn would be *her* family.

How did you tell someone you were his sister? Granted, it was Connor, one of her closest friends, but still. She wanted to do it right.

Armed with a laptop and a bowl of cereal, she crawled into bed and started on some research. Thanks to a bunch of online forums and chat rooms, she'd gathered heaps of information, read about people in similar situations and how they'd gone about connecting with their biological family.

That evening, after she'd bookmarked the last site and closed down the laptop for the night, her mind swung back to the physical part of her reality. In less than seven months, she'd be having a baby. The appointment she'd scheduled for next week loomed on the horizon, and suddenly her body went prickly with nervous tension.

She curled up in the bed, gently sweeping a hand over her belly. An official appointment. In writing. Out there.

It was really happening.

And Marco would be away for it.

She squeezed her eyes shut, refusing to let the guilt get to her. There was nothing she could do, right? He couldn't reschedule everything for her. It was as she'd said—just an ultrasound. There'd be plenty more opportunities for him to be involved.

Except she'd told him she didn't want him to be.

Did she even know what she wanted anymore?

Unable to answer that question, Kat buried herself in her work the next day, in the frantic energy of detailing Cyclone Rory's tragic path and sourcing stories that were all too depressingly bountiful now. Yet during their regular staff meeting when they argued the merits of each story and rearranged and reworked them for maximum viewer impact, she couldn't help but refocus on Marco's suggestion to follow her own dream.

A charity. A foundation where she would be in control, raise money and see each case through to completion from beginning to end.

So she began drafting a list, slowly filling in more details until she had two pages of handwritten notes. That night, during her usual hour on the treadmill, she reorganized it all in her head, until she finally had a semblance of a game plan. And the more she thought about it, the more excited she became. She'd even reached for her phone, eager to discuss it with Marco, but ended up balking at the last minute.

He was obviously busy, which was why he hadn't called.

She pressed the end button on the treadmill and grabbed her bottle, downing half the water as she cooled down. As amazing as it had been, the stupid sex thing had ruined it. She was thinking like a woman in a relationship, not as a best friend. Best friends didn't care who called whom first—they just *called*. They didn't stress about how many days, hours, minutes had passed since they'd spoken. And they certainly didn't let the other person get away with such a lengthy silence.

Just as she finally stepped off the treadmill and picked up her phone, it rang.

It was Connor. "Hey, stranger," she answered, way too cheerfully, as she grabbed her towel and walked into the kitchen.

"What are you doing tomorrow?" he asked.

"Saturday?" She jammed her phone under her chin then flicked on the hot water jug. "Oh, the usual. Watching TV. Eating by myself. Hiding from the hundreds of paparazzi camped on my doorstep."

"Where's Marco?"

"Swanning around in Darwin, I believe."

There was a pause as he picked up on her tone. "Did you guys have a fight?"

Kat sighed. "No, we are having…a difference of opinion."

"Anything to do with this engagement thing the press is going crazy with?"

She walked slowly back to her lounge room, clicked on the TV and muted the sound. "Partly. I just…" She sighed. "It's complicated. The baby. This press thing. Work. And I feel guilty that his appearances have been overshadowed by the media craving a sound bite. Did you know someone actually asked him about us during a ribbon cutting yesterday?"

"The press is full of idiots. Which is why I'm coming to see you."

She perched on the edge of her lounge. "If that were the real reason, you'd have come to see me way earlier than this."

His chuckle brightened her mood. "We'll lounge around and ignore the press together, eat pizza and watch *The X-Files*."

She couldn't help but smile. "Sounds divine."

"Or, you know, we could just go to Marco's island. Plenty of privacy there."

"God, don't you start. Next they'll be hooking you and me up instead of Marco."

He laughed again. "I dunno—I do like the sound of 'Kitco.' Much better than 'Markat.'"

"Shut up." When he laughed, she reluctantly joined him. "You're an idiot, Connor."

"Shh, don't tell anyone. You'll ruin my reputation."

She was still grinning when she hung up. Yes, her emotions were all over the place, and she had too many questions to ask and no idea how to approach Stephen… if she even wanted to. Frankly, the man scared the hell out of her and always had. But the one thing she had no issue with was accepting Connor as her brother. She loved him like a brother. More, actually, because she'd had years to appreciate him as a friend without any pressure or family obligation. As she walked down the corridor to the bathroom, she had to admit that she was looking forward to telling him. She had no idea how he'd react, but hopefully he'd feel the same way.

The next night, barely thirty minutes after she made it through her door with a relieved sigh, her intercom beeped.

"Chez Jackson?"

"I heard someone's having a pizza party."

She grinned at Connor's commanding voice. "Yep. With beer and juggling monkeys."

"I'm so there."

She buzzed him up and then unlocked the door. He stepped through the door five minutes later with an overnight bag, a steaming-hot Crust pizza and a huge grin.

"You are my savior." She hugged him then took the pizza and stepped back to allow him entry. He strode in with his usual lanky gait, his broad frame filling her space.

He dumped his bag near the couch. "Midnight must be a bit late for the paparazzi. I didn't see anyone about."

She shoved the pizza on the coffee table. "Oh, they're there—you just can't see them. Like cockroaches."

His laughter followed her as she went into the kitchen to get drinks and plates. When she emerged, he was scowling at his phone.

"What's up?" she asked.

"Everyone's got marriage on the brain." Connor slowly placed his phone on the table and sprawled on her couch. "My mother's been bugging me about it. Apparently a successful thirty-three-year-old guy needs a wife to appear more stable to our conservative European investors."

Kat patted his hand sympathetically. "Well, between Marco and me, I can honestly say it's not what it's cracked up to be."

Connor snorted. "Yeah. Two apiece, right?"

"I'm two. Marco is one and a half."

Connor centered a coaster on the table and placed his beer bottle on it. "So is there any truth to the rumors?"

"Which ones?" She flopped down on the single-couch chair.

"The marriage ones. Because everyone's waiting for the real press statement, you know, not the lame 'no comment' one."

"I know." She fixed him with a look. "Yes," she said at length.

"Yes, what? Marco actually asked you to marry him?"

"A few times, yes."

His breath came out in a whoosh. "Wow. And?"

Kat shook her head. "He only offered to avoid the nightmare PR—which is ironic, considering we're in the middle of it anyway. I haven't even announced I'm pregnant yet, so imagine what that'll do," she said as she flipped open the pizza lid and inhaled deeply. "Anyway, enough about that. I've got something more important to talk to you about. I need to—"

"Hang on, reverse." He leaned in. "More important than you being happy?"

"What?"

He sighed. "Can you not see it?"

"See what?"

He thumped a palm on the table. "You and Marco. You're perfect for each other."

Kat felt the tingle of embarrassment all the way down her spine, her eyes quickly darting away. "It's not like that, Connor. He's my—"

"Best friend, yeah, yeah, I know." Connor rolled his eyes. "You've both been preaching that old chestnut for so long, I'm ready to strangle someone. Why don't you guys just admit you love each other and put yourselves out of your misery?"

"I do love him, Connor. I love you, too."

He grinned. "Ditto, sweetheart. But you're not *in love* with me."

She frowned, the denial on her tongue, but instead she just pressed her lips together. "Look, forget that for a moment. I need to talk to you about something." She leaned in, hands tucked between her knees. "You know how I went for that blood test last month?"

Connor paused, midchew. "Yeah?" At her look he slowly placed the pizza on the plate, wiped his hands on a napkin and gave her his full attention. "Ah, Kat, don't tell me they got it wrong again...."

"No, nothing like that," she said quickly. "Okay, so the reason why my test was clear was...because... well..." It was still unbelievable, no matter how many times she tried to process it. Saying it aloud only made it more real. "Keith and Nina aren't my biological parents."

A deathly silence permeated her apartment.

Connor's brow dipped. "What?"

"I had a blood test. Nina and Keith are not my biological parents," she repeated patiently.

Connor's jaw dropped, eyes rounding. "No way."

Kat nodded. "It's true. My blood type and Mum's aren't compatible. Then we flew down to see my dad and he confirmed it."

"We? Marco went with you?"

She nodded. "And there's more."

He huffed out a breath. "Jeez, what?"

Kat smiled. "Connor..." She held his gaze unwaveringly. "My father is Stephen Blair."

Everything was still for a few seconds, maybe more, until Connor's loud bark of laughter split the air like a shot and she jumped. Frowning, she watched in silence as he sat there, chuckling and shaking his head. What did that mean? Was he...upset? Happy? Freaked out?

"Are you okay?" she finally said after a few moments.

He shot to his feet. "No, actually. Give me a moment."

She watched him pace, with one hand running through his hair, the other on his hip. It was worrying, not knowing if he'd taken the news as a good thing or not.

Finally, after a few interminable minutes, he turned to her. "You know, I just knew it was something like this. I *knew* it."

"What?"

He paused, taking in her expression, and shook his head. "About ten years ago, I caught the tail end of an argument. Couldn't hear much but I did eventually work out Mum and Dad were talking about a child. Oh, I didn't realize at the time that it was you," he hastened to add. "I never would've worked that one out."

She blinked. "What did they say?"

"Well, Mum was pretty pissed off—that was clear. Dad didn't want to talk about it, as usual. Then after, Mum ended up with a new Prada handbag and a necklace from Paspaley, and everything just seemed like normal."

Kat sat back in her chair, processing that information. "You didn't say anything about it to us."

Connor gave her a look. "I don't tell you guys everything."

True. Connor was extremely private when it came to his family—it had taken years for him to share even the most basic of details. It was only because they'd witnessed his parents' arguments firsthand that they knew about them at all. It was a deep source of embarrassment for him.

"Mum's always going on about Dad's affairs. You know that," he said now, picking absently at the label on his beer bottle.

Kat nodded, her expression solemn.

"So I overheard a bit more than usual. Apparently my mother still hasn't forgiven him for being in bed with another woman the day I was born."

Kat's mouth thinned. Connor projected such a hard and capable facade that people refused to believe there was a heart of gold under that swish Armani suit and classically handsome face. She knew that mask was to protect him from feeling too deeply, but she'd known him long enough to realize that he sometimes felt more than any of them put together.

"My sister, huh?" he said now, taking another swig of beer with a smile. "How do you feel about that?"

She was his sister. She had a *brother*. With everything else going on in her life, she'd pushed the impact of that detail to the back of her mind, but now, faced with a grinning Connor and the familiar way his eyes creased, the easily recognizable sweep of his nose, it was unmistakable.

She felt her mouth stretch into an answering grin. "Do we need to hug to mark this momentous occasion?"

"Hell, yeah." When he opened his arms, she got up, moved toward him and was enveloped in his embrace. The relief, the utter joy she felt at this moment, when it had just been bad news after bad news, was like a weight off her shoulders. She leaned into the hug, into his solid, hard warmth, and felt the tears well up. She couldn't believe how happy this actually made her.

Damn pregnancy hormones.

"Are you going to tell your dad that you know?" she asked, muffled against his shoulder.

He pulled back with a grimace. "I have no idea. After all these years of keeping the secret, do you think he'd want us to know? Plus, it could create a backlash with yours."

She nodded. "And it doesn't really change anything, him knowing, does it? I mean, I'm not going to demand in on the will or anything."

Connor laughed. "But it would be fun to call him Grandad in seven months' time." He glanced pointedly at her belly.

"You're terrible."

He laughed again, and again she felt the burden of the past few weeks shift.

Finally, something was going right. If only she could fix things with Marco.

Her expression must've given something away, because Connor's brow suddenly creased.

"Problem?"

"Oh, besides the gossip, pregnancy hormones and the fact Marco won't speak to me?"

"Well, you're not exactly speaking to *him,* are you?"

She opened her mouth to deny it but wisely closed it instead. "Plus his network contract's up for negotiation, so naturally they're speculating on that, too."

"They won't drop him. He's too much of a draw." Connor leaned back, cradling his beer with a small smile.

"What's that look for?"

"It's awesome you two are finally a couple. I always knew there was something, despite your denials."

"Connor, we're not. We're not speaking."

"Only because he's not here. Wait until you guys see each other again...next week, right?"

"Yes. At the awards thing."

"There you go. You'll be in Sydney, in a hotel. A

perfect opportunity to talk alone." When Kat remained silent, he impatiently tapped a finger against his bottle. "Listen. Is moping around with a head full of what-ifs better? No. Just say you love him, then kiss and make up."

"But I don't—"

"Sure you do."

"No…" *Yeah. You do.*

It was like a revelation. As if something fundamental had changed deep inside her. The false positive, the adoption, the baby had all added bit by bit to this moment, forcing her to see what was truly important in her life. To reassess again, to work out what was of true value to her.

The answer was so blindingly simple she gasped from the impact.

Marco. He was the one.

She sighed. "I told him we're just friends a few times, Connor," she said softly, voicing the doubt that had plagued her the past few days. "Surely there comes a time when he actually takes me at my word."

"You're talking about Marco here," Connor said. "And anyway, you're his best friend and you're having a baby together. He can't cut you out of his life permanently."

Kat nodded, saying nothing. Three times she'd pushed him back into the friends zone, and three times he'd not put up a fight.

Surely that said something?

She sighed, leaning back into the sofa. Either way, she'd have her answer next week.

She took a shaky breath. This was scary, so much scarier than anything she'd ever done in her life. Because in laying everything out there, there was a real possibility of rejection.

He could reject her. Say he just wanted to remain friends. And the question was, would she be satisfied with that?

Ten

The next five days were a crazy, breathless mess of activity. Kat was flat out at work, working on the Cyclone Rory stories, the follow-ups, the charity lines, but the overwhelming media attention on her personal life had started to impact on her work, with some sponsors severing their partnership at the last minute, leaving her frustrated and angry. Outwardly, Grace didn't seem overly concerned, but Kat knew she was furious. Couple that with their already cool tension, and work was not a pleasant place to be.

Marco had managed to call her once, the day of her ultrasound, but other than that, their texts had been short and sweet. And it broke Kat's heart, knowing their friendship was showing those irreversible cracks.

Finally something had to give. So the day before she

was due to fly to Sydney, she walked into Grace's office and firmly closed the door.

"I'll do it."

"Do what?" Grace asked, glancing up from stirring her morning coffee.

"The interview. An exclusive." She quickly put up a hand as Grace started to speak. "But everything—and I mean *everything*—has to go past me first."

Grace blinked slowly, then her face broke out into a huge grin as she shot to her feet. "Kat, this is brilliant! Wonderful! Oooooh…" She rounded the desk and embraced her in a cloud of perfume. "This has made my week…my month—hell, possibly my entire year!" Kat slowly pulled away, smiling thinly as her boss perched on the corner of her desk, beaming. "Can I ask you why now?"

Kat shrugged. "Timing. It's the right time."

Grace paused, watching her closely. "Really."

"Yep. Time to set the record straight once and for all. About everything." She met her boss's gaze unwaveringly, and in that small pause, an understanding passed between them, one that needed no words. This was Grace's moment and Kat was giving it to her. They both knew there'd never be another opportunity, just as they both knew things had fundamentally changed between them these past few weeks.

She knew it and Grace knew it.

"When?" Grace finally asked.

"Next week. After Sydney."

After another moment's pause, her boss nodded. "I'll set it up and let you know."

"Okay. And can you wait until after the awards before you start publicizing? The night should be about the players, not me," she added with a thin smile.

To her surprise, Grace nodded. "Sure."

"Thanks." Kat moved toward the door, unprepared for the wave of sadness that engulfed her. They both knew it wasn't just an interview date they were setting: it was Kat's quitting date, too.

Even knowing she was moving on to something bigger and better, something that really made her heart sing, didn't make leaving hurt any less. Despite the stress, the imperfections and the recent personal issues, this job had come at a perfect time, when she'd needed it the most. She'd always be grateful for that.

"Grace," she said now. "I want to thank you for—"

"No." The older woman shook her head, smiling softly as she reached for her ringing phone. "I thank *you*. It's been a pleasure working with you, Katerina Jackson."

Their gazes held for a moment, then Grace answered her call and it was Kat's cue to leave.

Kat flew into Sydney on Saturday and spent all day getting massaged, primped and fussed over, satisfied she'd gained at least some control over the spiraling situation. Meanwhile, Marco spent hours under harsh studio lights dressed in nothing but his underwear, fulfilling his Skins contract, so the first time they actually saw each other was half an hour before the limo picked them up for the FFA awards ceremony.

When she heard the knock at her hotel door, she nervously smoothed down her pale blue satin dress and pushed her hair behind her ears. All the half sentences she'd barely had time to practice crumbled on her tongue when she opened the door and saw him standing there, looking incredible and perfect in a designer suit and tie, his hair casually tousled and a familiar this'll-be-fun smile on his generous mouth.

His eyes swept over her thoroughly, taking in every last detail from her tight elaborate updo, to the dangling earrings and the strappy floor-length ice-blue ball gown with a respectable amount of ever-growing cleavage on show.

Then he held out his arm, said softly, "You look beautiful," and her heart just melted.

Twenty minutes later, stepping out of the limo onto the red carpet together, Kat took a moment to note the familiar players currently in European competition, now all returned for this special night that honored Australian-born sportsmen and women. As usual a smattering of die-hard and local fans stood behind the roped barriers, taking photos, and she felt her mouth curve, her expression calm.

She was ready to face the crowd.

She spent minutes gaining more confidence, her tension relaxing as she mingled with people she knew, chatting casually to old acquaintances.

This was going to be a good night, she thought as they made their way slowly down the carpet. No intrusive press, no focus on her. Just dinner and the awards. Yet as she turned, midsmile, and saw a familiar figure stride across the carpet, she faltered.

James Carter. James Bloody Carter.

Marco's former Marseille teammate, the Irish-born center who'd charmed her for over a year then convinced her to get married in a quickie Bali wedding. Then had promptly shagged some woman in their bridal suite seventy-two hours later.

It was too much to expect that he'd gotten fat and ugly in the years since she'd last seen him. If anything he was more handsome, more toned. Broader in the shoulders, leaner at the waist. His flashy suit set off a healthy physique so discreetly that to the untrained eye it might have seemed effortless. Kat knew better.

"What?" Marco was squeezing her arm, and she glanced up to see the concern in his face.

"James is here."

His mouth twisted briefly. "Really?"

She frowned, ignoring the fact they were on a red carpet with cameras within recording distance. "Wasn't he supposed to be in Italy or something?"

"Yeah." He took a step forward and they kept on walking. "Look, he's just a presenter. He'll be onstage most of the time, not at our table. He won't come over, and if he does, just say nothing."

"Easy for you to say. He's not the one who cheated on you."

Marco sighed. "Just…be cool, okay?"

She snorted. "I am *always* cool."

"Uh-huh."

He squeezed her hand, she grinned at him, and suddenly it was just as it was before, where they'd been so familiar, so close. So comfortable.

Damn, she missed that. It'd been three weeks since she'd seen him, and boy, she hadn't realized how much she'd missed him until he'd turned up at her door dressed in a formal suit and one of his expensive silk ties. And when he'd smiled…it had taken a massive effort not to tackle him then and there.

Now, with the heat rising in her belly, she glanced around at the smattering of people who'd stopped to rubberneck, the long red carpet that led into the plush foyer and the familiar faces of Sydney's football community. With a deep breath, she put on a smile and firmly shoved everything else from her mind. This was Marco's night, and she should just enjoy it. There was time enough for stress and worry later.

The ballroom easily seated two hundred and was elegantly decorated, with tiny blue downlights in the ceiling casting a cool glow over the round banquet tables. The tables themselves featured art deco–style centerpieces. People hovered around the bar, and a slide show above the stage was playing highlights of the past season backed by a classic-rock sound track.

Surprisingly, despite the presence of cameras and James, Kat was less tense than she thought she'd be. For one, the evening was about the awards and the players, not her. There were no intrusive questions or random photos or the usual stares-and-whispers from complete strangers. Sure, there were cameras, but she could smile nicely and handle a few shots. And as long as James kept his distance like he'd been doing for the past hour, she'd make it through the night unscathed.

She smoothed her gown down, thankful for the flowing empire style that hid her growing belly, only just managing to stop herself before placing a telling hand on the thirteen-week-old bump as she walked over to the bar. Even though this was a private function and she was fairly relaxed, everyone was still equipped with a camera and a Twitter account.

After she reached the bar and ordered drinks, she casually scanned the room, a small smile on her lips. A smile that immediately fell when she felt a guy stand-

ing way too close behind her. She frowned, preparing
to say something, but when she glanced back, all the
words just stuck in her throat.

"Hi there, Kitty."

James Carter was standing there, all casual as you
please, hands in his pockets, face creased into a charming grin. After darting her gaze around to see who was
watching—and seeing the coast was clear—she sent
him a withering look.

"What do you want?"

James's smile was perfect—too perfect. "What—no
hello? No 'how've you been these last few years?'" His
faint Irish accent oozed over her like thick molasses,
bringing with it a wealth of conflicting memories.

"I have nothing to say to you, James," she snapped.

His mouth quirked. "Is that any way to greet a long-
lost—"

"A long-lost what? A friend?" She snorted. "Let's
call it like it is. You're my cheating ex—a drinking
and gambling ex with a serious money-management
problem."

"Kitty, darlin'…" His expression was pained. "Don't
be like that. I didn't come over here to rehash old
wounds."

"Don't call me that." She frowned. "So why? You
want to give people *more* to talk about?"

"No." He drew a slow hand over his eyes. "But you're
kind of a one-woman pap magnet—the magazines and
papers are all over you. I flew in for the awards and—"

"I'm not interested in your life," Kat interrupted,
turning back to the bar.

As she waited for her order, she could feel his scrutiny. *Dammit, don't take the bait. Just ignore him, and then go back to Marco. Ignore it, ignore it. Ignore—*

With a sigh, she turned to him. "Fine. What do you want, James?"

"Forgiveness."

Kat blinked. "Sorry. Fresh out of that."

James took a step closer, and instinctively she stepped back against the bar. He winced. "Believe me, Ki-Kat. I'm truly sorry."

"Are you."

"Yes."

Kat flushed. "Well, 'sorry' doesn't cut it."

"What do you want me to say?"

"Nothing. Absolutely nothing." She nodded to the barman and then took the drinks.

"You know, after the divorce I spent a year working my way down to rock bottom," he began stiffly, following her as she made her way across the room. "I got into a car accident, spent forever in rehab. I'm a completely different person now."

She stopped. "I know. I read all about it." Briefly she recalled the headlines, the shock then relief she'd felt at reading about his struggles. "But I don't see what this has to do with me."

"I told you. I want to make amends."

"Fine. You've apologized. Now I'm going."

"Wait." His hand shot out, grabbing her elbow, and she stilled, staring at him.

Slowly he withdrew then self-consciously looked around at the clusters of noisy people milling about the room.

"You can't expect absolution just because you ask for it. This is so typical of you, James." She scowled.

"So selfish. I was your trophy girlfriend and then you cheated on me. There's no forgiving that."

"I know." His expression dropped, and for a second he looked genuinely contrite. "I can't excuse my past behavior."

"No, you can't."

She moved off, hoping he'd get the hint, but still he followed, until she got to her table and she finally put the drinks down.

James's mouth thinned in frustration. "You never let me explain. I wanted to talk on our honeymoon, but you stormed off. And anyway, you weren't such a saint yourself."

"What?"

"Yeah. You had this chip on your shoulder the size of Alaska. You carried around your toughness as if it were some goddamn bravery badge, instead of the defense it really was. And I always had to compete with Marco. The perfect, do-no-wrong, everybody-loves-me Marco Corelli."

"He is my *best friend!*"

"Really. Can you swear, right here and right now, that you never thought of him as more?"

"Of course not!" But she'd hesitated a second too long, and the look on James's face said it all.

"Did you sleep with him?"

She sucked in a sharp breath, gaze darting to the people around them. "Oh, my God, James, I am so not doing this with you. This is ridiculous!"

He glared at her, his handsome face twisted into angry lines, until he finally let out a breath, hand going to the back of his neck. "Look," he muttered, his gaze firmly on the floor. "I didn't come here to argue. I just wanted to—"

"You okay, Kat?"

Kat whirled, the words dying on her lips as her eyes collided with the steel of Marco's at the same time his arm looped loosely around her waist.

She was so stunned by the suddenly intimate gesture that she totally forgot to step away, to create a more platonic space between them. And Marco... Well, it was as if someone had cast a spell and turned him to stone, he was so still. Yet beneath that stillness, that cold expression, Kat could sense his body coiled as if he was ready to spring into action any second.

Dangerous.

"James," Marco finally said, his voice low and painfully polite.

James looked startled but swiftly recovered, holding out his hand. "Hi, Marco."

Marco slowly and pointedly looked at it and remained where he was. "Congratulations on your award. Player of the Year is quite an achievement."

James shot Kat a look of part frustration, part wariness. "Thank you."

She had to hand it to him—her ex was smooth. From the top of his expensively shaggy haircut to the soles of his shiny black dress shoes, the man had all the right props. He was someone who used charm and looks to get what he wanted.

When he flashed a perfect let's-all-be-friends-now smile, she couldn't suppress one of her own. *Oh, you're good, aren't you? So smooth. And Marco can see right through that.*

"So, Kat," James was saying, "we need to talk some more. I'm in room fourteen-oh-five."

"She won't be coming," Marco cut in smoothly before she could reply.

She gave him an irritated look then turned to James. "We've got nothing to discuss, James. End of story."

James scowled, his eyes going from Marco back to her. "Whatever you might think, Kat, I'd like to smooth out our differences. Start a clean slate."

A pause. Then, "Do you have a hearing problem?" Marco asked coolly.

"Butt out, Marco," James snapped. "This is between me and my wife."

"Ex-wife. She's my fiancée now. Oh, please, be my guest," he murmured as the other man clenched his fists.

"Fiancée? So you guys *are* getting married?" James's eyes widened, his gaze darting from Marco to her. "Huh. Guess that confirms things, then." As Marco bristled, he pulled himself up to his full six foot five and glared back.

Oh, for heaven's sake. It was like watching two dogs snarl and growl over a bone.

"No, we're not." She couldn't believe Marco had said the *F* word.

With a snort she moved out of Marco's embrace. "Okay, you need to leave now, James."

James sighed. "Look—" he stuck his hands on his hips "—I didn't want to do this here, but you leave me no choice. I've been asked to write my biography, a kind of inspirational, overcoming-the-odds thing. And I can't do it without mentioning you."

She sucked in a breath. "No."

James eyed Marco then came back to her. "Like it

or not, Kat, you were a part of my life. I'd like your approval on the chapter, but I can still publish it without your consent."

"James..." She took a deep breath, waiting for her brain to catch up. She could sue him, but that would take money and time, plus attract more attention to the book than it was worth. Or...

"If I don't like what I read, can I change it?"

"It depends what it is. But sure." He nodded. "I'm open to amendments."

That didn't mean a thing, but it was all he was offering. With a short nod, she said, "Fine. Email me the chapter when you have it."

James nodded and his mouth tweaked, a hint of what she used to think was the most devastating smile in the French soccer league.

She watched him leave in silence, her mind still halfway in the past. But at the last minute, as he was walking by the video tripod that had been filming the night, he abruptly turned.

"Congratulations on getting engaged," he called loudly, causing a few conversations to halt. "I knew that press release was a smoke screen—very clever. I hope you'll be happy. For what it's worth, I could totally see it coming."

A dozen people in earshot quickly turned to first James, then to Marco and Kat, and all of a sudden a chorus of cheery woo-hoos erupted.

No. Oh, no.

Kat's stomach bottomed out yet she refused to let it show. She simply shook her head at the closest group of well-wishers. "We're not... No, we haven't..."

Too late. The damage was done.

Embarrassment leached into a low, slow burn, one

that tightened her back, then her neck. She gritted her teeth, smilingly denied everything and stalked through the crowd, straight for the doors leading outside.

A handful of curses ran through her mind as she went. Damn James. Grace's exclusive was supposed to set everything straight, but now he'd gone and ruined it. Which meant they'd have to bring the interview forward.

Just as she dug out her phone and was about to reach the balcony doors, Marco grabbed her arm. "Kat. Stop."

"Marco…" She was barely holding it together, and his concern only tipped the scales.

She turned slowly to him with a dark frown. "Your fiancée?"

Marco shrugged, eyeing the people passing them by and giving them a casual nod. "I thought he needed a little encouragement to leave."

"With a lie?"

Marco studied her for a heartbeat. Then he said, "What upsets you more—the unwanted attention or me staking a claim?"

"You've no right to claim anything."

"Not even when you're having our baby?" he murmured.

Kat put a hand to the wall for support. Now that she was alone with Marco, she could no longer hold the memories at bay. They all came rushing back, making her skin heat and her head spin with remembrance. His lips and what they'd done to her. His warm breath, teasing her skin. And his wonderful hands, hands he now shoved aggressively in his pants pockets.

"Do you have any idea what this is going to do?" she said tightly. "How people are going to—"

"Going to what? Gossip?" A hand dived into his hair. "Christ, Kat, I'm really sick of hearing about it. I'm trying to help but you keep saying no. Stop complaining when you know you could fix it with one simple yes."

"Marco, this, on top of everything else...I just can't deal—"

"I know that." He leaned in, his face tight with anger. "I'm only guessing how things are for you because you haven't called, haven't wanted to discuss anything. It's like trying to get information from a goalpost."

She blinked, frowning. "Marco, I..."

"Look, this isn't the right place to talk," he said, curling his fingers around her wrist. "Let's go."

The automatic refusal was there, but she quickly swallowed it, giving him a brief nod. And when he turned and began to lead her firmly through the crowd, her breath quickened in anticipation.

This was it. They'd finally put it all out there. It would either be the end of their relationship or the beginning of one.

God, she was praying for the latter. Because the former would be like cutting a vital piece of her heart out.

There was no way she could do that. Ever.

Eleven

They stood in the middle of her hotel room barely ten minutes later, and as Kat watched him work his tie loose and slowly peel it off, everything just flew out of her mind.

It was incredible how her heart reacted to his presence. Her body just went all tingly, her blood heating as her eyes hungrily took in his broad frame, his strong cheekbones, his hair.

Everything.

When his gaze met hers, his expression was deadly serious. Not good.

He gestured. "You first."

She swallowed thickly. Could she honestly lay everything out in the open, finally? How on earth was she supposed to do that? Her nerves shook at the very thought.

And yet what was her alternative? Live with this painful ache, always wondering if things would have worked if she'd just had more courage to voice her feelings?

She barely had time to sort through her thoughts before he was right there, next to her, his expression unreadable.

She shoved her clutch onto the table and then threaded her fingers together, trepidation suddenly engulfing her. And all of a sudden she was left just staring at him, the words stuck in her throat. And that made her incredibly, annoyingly nervous.

"I'm waiting."

"I'm thinking."

"Okay." He crossed his arms and studied her, which made it that much worse.

"Stop looking at me!"

His eyes suddenly creased. "Sorry. Where would you like me to look?"

"Just… I don't know. Anywhere. The view." She waved to the window displaying a magnificent night panorama of Sydney Harbour. "You're making me nervous."

"That is not my intent, *chérie*."

She sighed. "I know. Look, there are a lot of things I have to get through and I wanted to tell you face-to-face, so you might want to take a seat, okay?"

"Is it the baby? Is everything all right?"

"Yes, it's fine. Everything is fine there." She took a deep breath, one that shook on the exhalation. "I was just reading about your contract negotiations."

He shrugged. "You know how the press likes to beat things up."

"So you're not going to move back to France, then?"

"It's one of many options on the table right now," he said cautiously.

"Right."

She let the silence fall, chewing on the inside of her lip as she tried to gather the right words.

He crossed his arms with a frown. "Kat, this isn't you, always second-guessing your words. Just come out and say it."

He was right. She'd handled more than her fair share of difficult situations. She could do this now. However she'd planned to do this, whatever preparations she'd made, this was it. She had to tell him.

And yet…her determination just seemed to crumble, making everything ache from the gaping hole it left. She may want to, so very badly. But it wouldn't be right. Or fair. Not when she was desperately in love with him but he just saw her as his best friend and marriage as a way to handle her PR nightmare.

She didn't want to marry him when he wasn't in love with her. That wasn't selfish, right? It was noble. It was good. It meant she cared for him way too much to see him unhappy.

Even if it killed her inside.

God, she was killing him! Marco's control had gone from torn to shredded in the space of a few moments as he sat there, waiting for her to say something, until he'd finally had enough.

"Kat." When he got abruptly to his feet, her surprised gaze followed him, and for another few seconds he chewed over the words, discarding a dozen imperfect ones, until he finally came up with everything he needed to say. "I love you."

She stilled, eyes wide, expression frozen for one horrible second. Then she shot out a soft breath and her small smile ripped at his heart. "I love you, too."

"No," he repeated, dragging in a breath. *Suck it up and just finish it already.* "No, I really love you."

"And I—"

"Kat, you are not getting it." He shook his head, heart thudding. "I am *in love* with you. I want to marry you, but not because of some press stunt, or out of any moral obligation. I want to marry you because I am desperately and hopelessly in love with you. I want to be with you, but only if you want that, too."

Shock didn't begin to describe the look on her face. She just stood there, silent and gaping, and for one horrible moment every terrible rejection he'd ever faced came bubbling up to the surface.

Her soft groan, the twisted expression, cut him swift and deep, but he could do nothing but stand there, waiting with his heart laid bare, waiting for her to let him down gently.

"I..." She floundered, frowning, then took a ragged breath.

"Kat..." he said, hating the way his voice came out all husky. "Say something. Anything."

Her eyes closed briefly, then opened again, and in that gaze he saw the truth. "These last few months— hell, these last few weeks—have been crazy for me. A baby, a pregnancy, this whole adoption thing. My head's been in ten different places, and I'm sick of it. Nothing is perfect, Marco, and I've just realized it doesn't have to be."

He remained silent, giving her nothing until she finished saying what she needed to say. He didn't have long to wait.

"It's taken all of this to make me see what is truly important," she said slowly, as if it was a revelation to herself, too. And when she reached out and took his hand, he offered no resistance, just let her link her fingers through his, the intimate glide of skin on skin sending his heart racing.

"And that's you. I don't want to spend the rest of my life wishing I'd had enough courage to tell you how I really feel, and I don't want to spend another day without being with you, talking with you. Loving you. If that means I only get you six months of every year, then, by God, I want those six months to count."

He closed his eyes as if her words had somehow cut, and Kat held her breath, waiting, waiting as the seconds ticked over.

"Dieu."

When he finally opened his eyes, the expression there had her going weak at the knees.

And suddenly, he was dragging her in for a kiss, a deep, hungry kiss full of emotion and feeling and heat. She squeaked in surprise then opened up for him, her arms going around his neck.

"Kat," he finally murmured against her mouth, hands slowly stroking her hair. "God, do you know how much I missed you these last few weeks?" Then he groaned, capturing her mouth for another kiss, and she was sure she was going to die from the joy of it all.

When he finally broke away, the look on his face was unmistakable. *"Je t'adore, chérie."* He cupped her cheek in his hand, placing his mouth softly on the corner of hers. "I've loved you for such a long time, but you've been so damn stubborn and I—" His breath caught in a growl and he kissed her again, a little more desperate, a little more hungry.

She whimpered against his mouth, her body pressed hard against his, every single inch of her skin tingling with awareness.

He loved her. How was that even possible? After everything she'd been through, how on earth had she managed to score this amazing, wonderful guy—her best friend—as her lover, as well?

"Come here."

She led him into her bedroom then closed the door, her entire body beating out a loud pulse as her blood rushed to every corner. With a trembling hand she shoved her fingers under his shirt and swept the outline of his ribs. After she lifted his shirt, she followed with her lips, kissing softly.

She took a deep breath, trying to calm her nerves, but it only succeeded in filling her lungs with his unique scent. "You smell amazing."

His chuckle did crazy things to her gut. "Thanks. You don't smell so bad yourself."

She grinned against his skin, her lips grazing across his hip, her hand curling around the other. "Is that a murmur of appreciation I hear?"

"Yeah." His guttural response made her flush and smile. "Kat..."

"Yes?"

"Stop talking."

When she began to mouth her way slowly across to his navel, he groaned and relaxed back on the couch, her kisses flaming a path while she stroked his hip and he muttered in Italian. He had the most perfect voice. Perfect hands. Perfect everything.

"You're perfect," she muttered against his skin.

"No…" he ground out.

"Yes," she countered. "And this part, right here—" her hand skimmed over the defined muscular V-line flanking his hips, the Adonis belt "—is such a temptation."

"Yeah?" His breath came out in a rush as she continued to stroke.

"Yes. Just above your waistband. Drives me crazy every time."

"How crazy?"

"Like this." Quickly she unsnapped his jeans and placed her mouth on the spot, softly trailing her lips over the muscle, before heading back to the center, tracing the thin line of hair downward.

His sharp breath as she finally eased his jeans down fueled her already stoked fire. He raised his hips a little to help, and when she'd tossed his pants aside, she couldn't help but swallow thickly at the sight of him lying there.

Wanting *her*.

"Kat…" It was only one word, yet the raw vulnerability behind it made her heart contract.

She slid her hands up along his corded thighs, gripping his hips, and then took him in her mouth with firm command. When his hips bucked, she placed a steady hand on his stomach.

"Shh." She continued to pleasure him, reveling in the heady power and the wonderful hard-velvet feeling of having him in her mouth.

And when she felt his body finally tense, she stopped.

His gasp and obscene curse echoed loudly. "Kat? What the hell?"

She slid up, her naked body gliding against him, and she stopped to nibble on his bottom lip briefly before straddling him.

"Impatient," she muttered against his mouth.

"Tease."

"No way." Eyes locked on his, she positioned her hips then swiftly eased down on him with a sharp breath.

They moved together in perfect time, two people in love, experiencing joy in each other, reveling in the pure physical moment. And when everything just became too much, her emotions so overwhelming she couldn't take any more, her release crashed in a wave of pure ecstasy, leaving her trembling and spent. With a soft groan, Marco followed her, his arms wrapped tight, holding her in place as their damp bodies slid together as one.

The minutes ticked by, the thick air punctuated by their ragged breathing. Kat lay there, soaking up his heat, a thousand words on the tip of her tongue but reluctant to say a thing because she didn't want to shatter this most perfect moment.

But finally, as their bodies cooled and their heartbeats returned to normal, Marco glanced over at the clock on the bedside table and said, "Maybe we should be getting back to the ceremony…"

Kat followed his gaze. "I guess."

He chuckled. "So enthusiastic."

"Well, given the choice, I know where I'd rather be."

"I know how you feel."

They remained perfectly still, as the moment stretched.

"Marco…" Kat finally said. "I'm quitting my job."

A pause. "Really?"

She nodded, glancing up at him. "I'm going to start up a charity. Not sure what, yet. I'll think about it while I'm busy with being pregnant." She smiled faintly.

When his hand slid to her stomach, palm moving possessively over the gentle swell, her breath caught. Then he smiled and leaned down to kiss her, and everything just choked her up all over again.

"I don't want you to overdo things," he murmured softly against her mouth.

"I can hire people. Delegate."

He spent a few moments lazily kissing her. "So you really want to do it?"

"Do you think I *can* do it?"

"*Chérie,* you can do anything you want."

She basked in the warmth of his smile, until seconds passed and realization began to seep in.

"Sooooo…" she said softly. "About that marriage thing—"

"Yes?"

"Is the offer still on the table?"

He blinked. "No."

"What?" She frowned.

He cupped her face, brought her to his mouth in a gentle kiss. "It's not a business offer. I am asking you to be my wife. To be with me for the rest of our lives. To have my children, to make me happy and to let me make you happy. It's a marriage proposal made with love."

Oh. Breathless, all she could do was stare at him, at the tender look in his dark eyes, at the curve of his mouth. And she fell in love with him all over again.

That was…absolutely perfect. More than perfect.

It was Marco.

She felt the tears well a second before he reached

out and caught one on the tip of his finger, his smile gently warming her.

"Tears, *chérie*?"

She sucked in a breath. "It's the hormones."

"Sure. Not tears of happiness?"

She sniffed, blinking furiously. "Maybe." At his look, she laughed, a weird watery sound. "Probably."

"I know." His kiss was tender, soft and everything she could have wanted to mark this moment. "So," he breathed against her lips, "will you marry me?"

"Of course I will," she replied without hesitation. "You're my best friend. My Marco. I love you."

"And I love you. My Kat."

* * * * *

Don't miss these other stories from
Paula Roe:
THE PREGNANCY PLOT
BED OF LIES
PROMOTED TO WIFE?
THE BILLIONAIRE BABY BOMBSHELL

All available now, from Harlequin Desire!

REQUEST YOUR FREE BOOKS!
2 FREE NOVELS PLUS 2 FREE GIFTS!

HARLEQUIN®

Desire

ALWAYS POWERFUL, PASSIONATE AND PROVOCATIVE

YES! Please send me 2 FREE Harlequin Desire® novels and my 2 FREE gifts (gifts are worth about $10). After receiving them, if I don't wish to receive any more books, I can return the shipping statement marked "cancel." If I don't cancel, I will receive 6 brand-new novels every month and be billed just $4.55 per book in the U.S. or $4.99 per book in Canada. That's a savings of at least 13% off the cover price! It's quite a bargain! Shipping and handling is just 50¢ per book in the U.S. and 75¢ per book in Canada.* I understand that accepting the 2 free books and gifts places me under no obligation to buy anything. I can always return a shipment and cancel at any time. Even if I never buy another book, the two free books and gifts are mine to keep forever.

225/326 HDN F4ZC

Name _____ (PLEASE PRINT) _____

Address _____ Apt. # _____

City _____ State/Prov. _____ Zip/Postal Code _____

Signature (if under 18, a parent or guardian must sign)

Mail to the Harlequin® Reader Service:
IN U.S.A.: P.O. Box 1867, Buffalo, NY 14240-1867
IN CANADA: P.O. Box 609, Fort Erie, Ontario L2A 5X3

Want to try two free books from another line?
Call 1-800-873-8635 or visit www.ReaderService.com.

* Terms and prices subject to change without notice. Prices do not include applicable taxes. Sales tax applicable in N.Y. Canadian residents will be charged applicable taxes. Offer not valid in Quebec. This offer is limited to one order per household. Not valid for current subscribers to Harlequin Desire books. All orders subject to credit approval. Credit or debit balances in a customer's account(s) may be offset by any other outstanding balance owed by or to the customer. Please allow 4 to 6 weeks for delivery. Offer available while quantities last.

Your Privacy—The Harlequin® Reader Service is committed to protecting your privacy. Our Privacy Policy is available online at www.ReaderService.com or upon request from the Harlequin Reader Service.

We make a portion of our mailing list available to reputable third parties that offer products we believe may interest you. If you prefer that we not exchange your name with third parties, or if you wish to clarify or modify your communication preferences, please visit us at www.ReaderService.com/consumerchoice or write to us at Harlequin Reader Service Preference Service, P.O. Box 9062, Buffalo, NY 14269. Include your complete name and address.

HD13R

"Colleen!"

That deep voice was unmistakable. Colleen had been close to Sage Lassiter only one time before today. The night of his sister's rehearsal dinner. From across that crowded restaurant, she'd felt him watching her. The heat of his gaze had swamped her, sending ribbons of expectation unfurling throughout her body. He'd smiled and her stomach had churned with swarms of butterflies. He'd headed toward her, and she'd told herself to be calm. Cool. But it hadn't worked. Nerves had fired, knees weakened.

And just as he had been close enough to her that she could see the gleam in his eyes, J.D. had had his heart attack and everything had changed forever.

Sage Lassiter *stalked* across the parking lot toward her. He was like a man on a mission. He wore dark jeans, boots and an expensively cut black sport jacket over a long-sleeved white shirt. His brown hair flew across his forehead and his blue eyes were narrowed against the wind. In a few short seconds, he was there. Right in front of her.

She had to tip her head back to meet his gaze and when she did, nerves skated down along her spine.

"I'm so sorry about your father."

A slight frown crossed his face. "Thanks. Look, I wanted to talk to you—"

"You did?" There went her silly heart again, jumping into a gallop.

"Yes. I've got a couple questions…."

Fascination dissolved into truth. Here she was, day-dreaming about a gorgeous man suddenly paying attention to her when the reality was he'd just lost his father. As J.D.'s private nurse, she'd be the first he'd turn to.

"Of course you do." Instinctively, she reached out, laid her hand on his and felt a swift jolt of electricity jump from his body to hers.

His eyes narrowed further and she knew he'd felt it, too.

Shaking his head, he said, "No. I don't have any questions about J.D. You went from nurse to millionaire in a few short months. Actually, *you're* the mystery here."

Read more of
THE BLACK SHEEP'S INHERITANCE,
available April 2014
wherever Harlequin® Desire and ebooks are sold.

Desire

ALWAYS POWERFUL, PASSIONATE AND PROVOCATIVE.

ONCE PREGNANT, TWICE SHY
Red Garnier

What's one impulsive night between old friends?

Tied together by tragedy, wealthy Texan tycoon
Garret Gage promised to protect family friend Kate
just as fiercely as her father would have. And he'd been
doing just fine until one night of passion and a secret
changes everything.

Look for
ONCE PREGNANT, TWICE SHY
by Red Garnier April 2014 from Harlequin® Desire!

Wherever books and ebooks are sold.

Also by Red Garnier
WRONG MAN, RIGHT KISS

HD73311

HARLEQUIN®

Desire

ALWAYS POWERFUL, PASSIONATE AND PROVOCATIVE.

HIS LOVER'S LITTLE SECRET
Billionaires and Babies
by Andrea Laurence

She's kept her baby secret for two years...

But even after a chance run-in forces her to confront the father of her son, Sabine Hayes refuses to give in to shipping magnate Gavin Brooks's demands. His power and his wealth won't turn her head this time. But Gavin never stopped wanting the woman who challenged him at every turn. He has a right to claim what's his...and he'll do just about anything to prevent her from getting away from him again.

Look for HIS LOVER'S LITTLE SECRET
by Andrea Laurence April 2014, from Harlequin® Desire!

Don't miss other scandalous titles from the
Billionaires and Babies miniseries,
available now wherever ebooks are sold.

DOUBLE THE TROUBLE by Maureen Child
YULETIDE BABY SURPRISE by Catherine Mann
CLAIMING HIS OWN by Elizabeth Gates
A BILLIONAIRE FOR CHRISTMAS by Janice Maynard
THE NANNY'S SECRET by Elizabeth Lane
SNOWBOUND WITH A BILLIONAIRE by Jules Bennett

HD73308